SKYDIVING ON CHRISTOPHER STREET

by Stan Leventhal

ReQueered Tales
Los Angeles • Toronto
2021

Skydiving
on Christopher Street

by Stan Leventhal

ReQueered Tales version 1.42
Kindle edition ASIN: B08VDKNJVQ
Epub edition ISBN-13: 978-1-951092-34-4
Print edition ISBN-13: 978-1-951092-35-1

*For more information about current and future releases,
please contact us:*

E-mail: *requeeredtales@gmail.com*
Facebook (Like us!): www.facebook.com/ReQueeredTales
Twitter: @ReQueered
Instagram: www.instagram.com/requeered
Web: www.ReQueeredTales.com
Blog: www.ReQueeredTales.com/blog
Mailing list (Subscribe for latest news): https://bit.ly/RQTJoin

Praise for
SKYDIVING
ON CHRISTOPHER STREET

"A tender, honest novel about that moment between diagnosis and the decision to grow. Messy boyfriends and dreamy crushes set against the back-drop of daily life make Leventhal's characters vulnerable and familiar. His insider's view of the porn industry adds a comically surprising dimension."

— Sarah Schulman,
Let the Record Show: A Political History of ACT UP New York

"Stan Leventhal's new novel, *Skydiving on Christopher Street*, is a startling attempt to capture the life of an urban gay man on the printed page. Like Christopher Isherwood's *A Single Man*, the book relies on plain-spoken language to convey the depth and multiplicity of lived experience. Read in conjunction with Leventhal's earlier *Mountain Climbing in Sheridan Square*, the book moves us into a darker, more disturbing arena in which knowledge does not necessarily bring happiness, understanding does not bring relief. But in spite of this, Leventhal's vision is clear and undaunted. For all of its somber chiaroscuro, *Skydiving on Christopher Street* challenges us to see the world through new eyes and to revel in its author's ability to translate life into art, pain into understanding."

— Michael Bronski,
A Queer History of the United States

Also by **STAN LEVENTHAL**

Mountain Climbing in Sheridan Square (1988)

A Herd of Tiny Elephants (1988)

Faultlines (1989)

The Black Marble Pool (1990)

Candy Holidays and Other Short Fictions (1991)

Skydiving on Christopher Street (1995)

Barbie in Bondage (1996)

SKYDIVING ON CHRISTOPHER STREET

by Stan Leventhal

Table of Contents

On the Page:
The Real Stan Leventhal
in his Literary World

When I decided that I wanted to meet Stan Leventhal in person, it was already impossible. I was a fairly subdued high school student in New Delhi, India. It was the year 2000. My only exposure to anything gay in images were Jonathan Demme's *Philadelphia* and a fashion designer that had just come out publicly. My knowledge of AIDS came from public service documentaries that were almost entirely focused on the aspect of sexual transmission. The message seemed to be that it is a disease that only dirty sexual people catch.

I chanced upon a copy of the *Skydiving on Christopher Street*, wrapped in plastic at a newsstand next to a video store that I would frequent. It was buried under a towering pile of throwaway pulp and comics, some even used. This said nothing, of course, about the merit of the book, but did not bode well for the space for queer literature in what was then my neck of the woods. There were literary circles for the LGBTQ community, there were "special nights" at clubs to meet and engage in person, but there wasn't quite an acceptable vocabulary for the things "they" did, wrote or read about. I picked up the copy for about 2.50 dollars and snuck it into a plastic bag with a DVD of Tobe Hooper's *Poltergeist*. This edition by Hard Candy Books had a bare-chested male model on the cover, and that - along with the blurbs about porn publishing as the setting - meant to me that it could well be pornographic in nature.

That night opened up a whole new world for me.

I was aware that the word for what I was, was perhaps

"gay", but the world of Stan's story had much more to say about love, strength and survival than I imagined. It was not just a defense against the unfortunate association of a disease with the gay community that shaped much of public perception. The unnamed protagonist was somebody Stan knew inside out. I discovered nearly two decades later, that his last two novels were, in fact, very much semi-autobiographical. Like Stan, the narrator edits stories for an erotic magazine to make a living. Like Stan, he is part of a writers circle. Like Stan and many of his contemporaries, he has been diagnosed HIV positive. He has not only lost friends and lovers to AIDS-related complications, but he's struggling to sustain the old, while trying to build new, relationships amidst uncertainties, amidst a lack of political will on part of the Bush administration to fund initiatives that could help save lives. But most of all, he is much like Stan, an incredibly well-read and discerning citizen, a beacon, and a nurturer of other writers.

A fervent cinephile by that time, and perhaps only twenty pages in – I pledged to adapt the book into a feature screenplay because it seemed vivid in its deceptive simplicity, comforting in its conversations with the reader, and dialogue between people living in that world with relatable hindrances: tyrant and offensive bosses, families that you love to hate, and memories that are just as much an oasis of solace as a nexus of remorse and regret.

Through the course of this deeply personal narrative, the protagonist finds himself in a world that he has fought hard to be part of. Yet this very world won't spare him a day when he doesn't have to battle his supervisors, when he doesn't have to deal with an apartment building that's as much in shambles as his relationship with his Broadway boyfriend, when he doesn't have to turn to the past for comfort. It is a world that he chose, but one that threatens to evict him at any moment. As much as it is an occupational hazard – going over strange mail from subscribers, requests to meet some of the porn stars featured in the magazines, dealing with threats and indictments, mind-numbing interviews with models and scanning photo slides of objectified bodies – much of the humor and insight come from these workplace episodes where "porn is political". He struggles to stay grounded in the present, but the past is only accessible in voices and whiffs, songs and words.

Deftly lilting between the gritty and the ethereal, I hadn't yet heard an author's voice so appealing and soothing – in deep contrast to the often shaky universe of the plot. For all the lack of clarity that the narrator experiences, there is a coherent quality to the telling of the story itself, arguably misunderstood as lacking innovation. The book became my bedside companion for years to come. I wasn't dealing with an epidemic, I wasn't even in America, but nearly everything spoke to me, especially the nature of fleeting romantic relationships in a world that refuses to stay still. In the strangest ways, it mirrored so much of my own life. Therein, perhaps, is just one small testament to the potentially wide appeal of this book's narrative.

Stan had been gone five years by the time that I discovered this book. Yet, thanks to a blog post that I wrote in 2013, a serendipitous turn of events in Los Angeles put me in touch with the fiery and compassionate Michele Karlsberg, one of his best friends. No sooner, I found myself face-to-face with Stan's brother Gary Lee, discussing the idea of the book as a movie.

The conversation between Gary and I turned into an act of fond remembrance between two people that had known him in very different ways. One was related by blood and shared many a night with him during their college years in Boston. As Gary recalls, "If it weren't for him, my taste in music might not be what it is today. He was my best friend. I loved going to concerts with him. And, when we were kids, he often included me in things he was doing with his friends. That's just who he was." They listened to everything from The Who and Frank Zappa to The Weavers and Judy Collins. The other was a screenwriter that had known him merely through his words, anecdotes from people that lived through that time with him, through comprehensive essays by another of his great friends, Sarah Schulman and a volume by Edmund White. In that moment, indeed, Stan Leventhal manifested as close as he could to flesh and blood: (much like the specters in the book) the kid that fervently produced his own little music magazine called The Folk Bag, the firebrand that went to marches against the war in Vietnam, someone persuasive enough with his parents to get high within the walls of the house, someone that temped at a theater box office while writing his own work and reviewing others. A lot of that Stan you can also find in *Skydiving on Christopher Street*: enterprising, activist, assertive, creative - but also weakened by a condition of unprecedented impact. You see him as one of the lovers on their own separate paths. As a porn editor, he is torn between what could be meaningful and what is a merely functional enterprise. This is a dilemma that he seemed to have tackled at Out Write, the first gay and lesbian writers conference at San Francisco in 1990. He responded decisively to one of the audience pondering the choice between writing "safe" erotica versus the purely erotic: "The bottom line is always the artistic one, not the political line. And when I'm reading a story and deciding if I'm gonna buy it or publish them, I don't care if there's a condom in the story or not. What I care about is, does the story arouse me sexually?"

If, like Christopher Bram says in his introduction to *Mountain Climbing on Sheridan Square*, the experience evokes something akin to hanging out with Stan's friends and circle, reading this book is like shadowing him, letting you hear every thought in his head as he gets closer to morbidity and meditates on its nature, while also celebrating the life that is and once was, as he takes a redemptive journey from anhedonia to enthusiasm, from despair to hope, from guilt to pride. None of those could be alien to any of us.

One of the most poignant (and possibly cinematic) moments in the book is when the narrator rides a cab through the rapidly gentrified New York of the early '90s, with a box full of things that his ex-boyfriend has left behind in their former apartment. He is struck here, as if for the first time, by how the city has been effaced by a newness he is yet to fully comprehend, let alone embrace. Midway through the chapter he realizes those things were intentionally left behind for him, not merely forgotten in a rush. He talks of a "renewed ease" in the relationship. This mélange of dreamy realism is part of the sensitive and empathetic Stan that most will describe.

At a time when a new pandemic has been unleashed by the not so novel coronavirus, and we hear accounts of how certain neighborhoods around America are reminded of the bleakness of the AIDS crisis, I am only more certain that *Skydiving on Christopher Street* can shield us a little from the apprehensions and uncertainties that we're faced with, bring us comfort with its testament of communities helping fellows endure pain: all that, while it celebrates little joys, finds humor in dire circumstances. As is evident from his books, Stan was also deeply aware that the idea of kinship during tough times begins with forgiving oneself, and the realization that no one has, and will ever – have it easy.

As I labor on with the screen story for this understated marvel, it brings me great relief and tremendous joy to witness that Stan's work has endured and still holds the potential to offer retrospection, reflexiveness and comfort to its readers, no matter the context.

— Paras Borgohain,
September, 2020

Paras Borgohain is a screenwriter for diverse audiences, including eight broadcast seasons of Sesame Street and a feature for Turner Broadcast International. He was a 2016 BlueCat Screenplay Award recipient, and one of the twelve writers recommended for the Scriptapalooza Screenwriting Fellowship in 2017 - both in recognition of his queer epistolary drama Deepest, Darkest or How Not to Lie. He is currently developing two feature screenplays and a limited miniseries.

This book is dedicated to the loving memory of

Bobby Nolen Locke, forever and always.

ONE

I CLOSE MY EYES.

To rest them for a while.

And I see a picture, slightly out of focus. It's not entirely motionless like a painting or photograph. Nor is it filmlike with movement. I know I'm not dreaming. Human figures, vaguely resembling friends and acquaintances, stand on pure air midway between the ground and sky. Buildings and trees also defy gravity and logic. There are waves and particles in the air, as though the atmosphere is like an ocean. I can see motes and unidentifiable flotsam, drifting like plankton, at the mercy of uncontrollable forces. Moon pull. The push of orbital motion. I cannot quite grasp anything. The watery consistency is impossible to hold. The shifting patterns, like quicksilver, will not be contained by my senses. I open my eyes.

There is no escape.

Jon comes home from work. And asks me how my day was, casually dressed and aloof in his manner. With a dark and brooding look when he's not smiling, his hair always perfect, the brown eyes that shimmer and pull me in have a strong grasp.

"The usual bullshit," I count three beats, knowing this song so well, "and how was yours?"

"More of the same." He pouts and removes his jacket. An expensive leather number with the logo of a hit Broadway show emblazoned across the back.

I wait for his speech. The one he delivers to remind me of his importance, and tacitly, of my insignificance.

"Well," he begins, sitting, untying the laces of his high-tops, "we had a special rehearsal today to break in the new understudy and, of course, I was the only one who paid any attention because everyone else was stoned or hung-over."

He flashes his self-satisfied, self-righteous grimace and I stare at him, expressionless, always at a loss when trying to respond to his boasting. He takes a cigarette pack from his jacket pocket, removes the cellophane and tosses it on the floor. As though the apartment were his personal trash can. I look at the wrapper on the floor and then raise my eyes to look at his face. I perform this motion with as much obviousness as possible. From the floor to his face, from his face to the floor and back again.

"Are you going to just leave it there?" I finally ask, because if I don't bring this to his attention I'll be forced to pick it up and throw it away myself, and in the process, sacrifice what little dignity I have left.

He looks at me as though I've just accused him of raping my grandmother. Angry and glowering, with venom in his eyes, he stoops to pick up the wrapper and tosses it in the trash receptacle. "Fuck you!" he spits at me, then marches to the bathroom. Slams the door.

This is my punishment for reminding him that he's a human being, not a god, and that good human beings who have attained some degree of maturity clean up after themselves.

Now I'll get the silent treatment for the rest of the evening.

The apartment is too small for me to go elsewhere within it. It consists of one medium-sized room, and a tiny one the size of a closet. So I remain on the couch, containing my anger. And when he emerges from the bathroom I pretend I'm not there. I open a book and start reading. He plays a CD of musical climaxes from low-budget horror films. Both of us pretend the other is not here. Life has been proceeding like this for about two years. I don't know how much longer I can withstand the long empty silences, the harsh recriminations.

The music confounds my concentration. A lot of loud clashes with kettle drums thundering and trumpets blaring. The strings add microtonal punctuation. I close the book and try another. But I cannot follow the words. I close my eyes. Jon is whirling in mid-air as I stand off to the side watching. The mistakes of my past, my ex-lovers, parade across the bottom of the picture, reminding me that I have never been lucky or successful with live-in, long-term relationships. I open my eyes and watch Jon conducting the horror film orchestra. And wonder if the ghost of my father is watching me. Does he know that Jon is making me sad? Does he care? Does he think me a fool who deserves what he gets? Or does he pity me for getting involved with the wrong person?

I realize I'll never know what he would think if he could see all the things I do. I want to cry. But not with Jon present. I hold everything back. Attempt to read some more. I can't.

It's Monday night, the theater's dark, I have nowhere to go, we're stuck with each other.

"Anything good on television?" I ask, gently, to soften the silence like a brick wall between us.

Jon glares at me. Still angry. Not speaking.

"We could rent something from the video store," I add.

"Shut up! Can't you see I'm trying to listen?"

"Sorry."

Then I close my eyes and try to imagine my life if Jon were somebody else, or if he lived somewhere else. Anywhere else.

Every workday morning I face a long dark corridor. Having ridden up in the elevator, I switch off the alarm system and open the office. I suppose it's some measure of my reliability and honesty that I've been entrusted with the keys. And the alarm code. I like getting to work early. It's quiet and peaceful. I walk from the reception area to the time clock, then to my cubicle, turning on all the lights. Later, when everything is a mad hustle, I'll yearn to leave. But in the gentle, silky morning, I feel like there's nowhere else to be.

I play the role of receptionist until Rita arrives. Sitting at the phone console, with the message slips and package logs, I'm like the king of all I can see. I control the communications system, therefore, I am in the power seat. There are five calls before nine o'clock. Often I get heavy breathers who hang up as soon as they hear my voice. What turns them on is the feminine purr of Rita's alto; my baritone is not what they've been dreaming about.

I read a book or magazine; the secretaries and subscription department personnel begin to arrive. The serenity is shattered as good mornings and how are yous ricochet down the halls. The phone rings with increasing frequency, legitimate business persons and customers trying to connect.

Where's Rita? She's supposed to arrive by eight-thirty but it's almost nine. I get bored with all the meaningless morning chatter. It's a hot summer day, everyone emerges from the elevator, shakes his or her head and says, sure is hot! It's sweltering out there! Having just come from there myself this is not news. It's redundant, obvious, and makes me long for something a bit more substantial. Interesting. During the winter months it's the same thing. As my ears thaw and my fingers push away the numbness, I'm assaulted with a chain of mundane comments on the temperature, the wind. I'd probably fall out of Rita's chair if anyone greeted me with something original, clever, witty, noteworthy or surprising.

I'm tempted to mock them. Respond to their innocent remarks with scathingly sarcastic rejoinders. But I don't. I'm pleasant and amiable. And so begins another day of deception. Success in modern American business depends largely on how willingly, easily, and convincingly you can lie. Tell people what they want to hear instead of the truth. If you have not learned how to tell a credible lie your chances for success are meager, your likelihood to fail almost inevitable.

Prior to Rita's arrival, I've already told approximately twenty-five lies. Saying that I feel fine when actually I'm tired, cranky, pissed-off, or depressed, saying I had a wonderful weekend though I was bored beyond belief. When Rita finally appears, the numbers increase with alarming speed.

"Good morning, sugar!" she says with far too much enthusiasm, twisting and turning like a model on a runway, expecting me to comment on her spiffy threads. She's short, slim, adorable. Prominent cheekbones. Skin as dark and smooth as polished mahogany.

"Good morning!" I respond, hoping my forced cheer isn't too obvious. And though every fiber of my being wants to ignore her desperate plea to be noticed, her need for a compliment, I add, "What a lovely blouse! And that skirt. It's perfect for you."

She is pleased even though I've said nothing about her hair. I hate myself for acknowledging that the green blouse and brown skirt are anything more than devices to keep the body warm, prevent the wearer from being arrested for indecent exposure.

"What did you do last night?" she asks. And before I can reply, tells me about her evening, which is the reason why she asked me, having no genuine interest in how I spend my time, but eager to tell everyone how she spends hers. I pretend to have great interest in her boyfriend Fred, the cookies and ice cream they ate, the reruns of old sitcoms they watched, the beer they drank later, the argument which led to a long night alone.

I try to make my sympathetic response sound as sincere as possible, and before she can milk me for more, quickly add that I should get to my desk and start working.

"See you later," she chimes, her hand-mirror already staring at her face, one hand adjusting her hair.

"Later."

My cubicle is about the size of a broom closet. There is a plastic desk with fake wood paneling, a couple of shelves, a gray file cabinet and a red typewriter. Like the rest of the complex, the walls are off-white, the carpet speckled aquamarine. The speckles are from the workmen who spilled paint and grease, ground out cigarette butts, spat chewing gum. When the offices were renovated management arranged for the carpeting to be laid prior to the other heavy work that had to be done. The consequence being that the newly purchased wall-to-wall looks old, worn, and does not quite convey the intended impression. Prosperity is indicated by gleaming neatness and cleanliness, a slovenly appearance points toward failure. The managers of this firm do everything backwards. There is no logic, little common sense, a paucity of planning and imaginative thinking.

I place a piece of paper in the typewriter and mentally prepare myself to write a letter to the editor. Me. I write all of the letters to the editor. I've been doing this for over three years now but so far not one of the thousands, possibly millions, who read the magazines have picked up on this. Magazine publishing, like Hollywood moviemaking, is about illusion. Just like the fake outdoor and city street backdrops, the plastic surgery, the high-tech special effects, and the publicists' claims that the starring actor is heterosexual, little that occurs in the pages of most periodicals is as it appears.

I start typing. A message long on hyperbole proclaiming how wonderful the May issue of *Big Boys* is. How glorious the naked model on page eighty-seven. How delightful the jerk-story on page thirty-two. I sign the letter, (P.W., Seattle, WA,) and pause to decide which glowing encomiums to utilize, and which city and state will close the next letter.

But before I can resume typing, the head of the subscription department appears and bids me "Good morning!"

Jeannette is a diminutive Asian-American woman with straight black hair, small breasts, and very expressive hands. She pops into my cubicle and asks me about my night. Before I can reply she tells me all about the same sitcom reruns that Rita and her boyfriend watched.

I listen dutifully, inserting all of the appropriate reallys, no kiddings, you don't says, and wows. Then I excuse myself, laying the blame on my unbelievable workload, the letters to the editor taking the rap.

A few seconds later, Joseph, one of the assistant vice presidents, appears. He's got a jiggly paunch, sagging jowls, and his eyes always look bloodshot. "What did you do last night?" he asks, poised to tell me everything I don't want to hear.

"Not much," I say, thinking that not only would he be uninterested in what I have to share about Nin and Boccaccio, but he's probably never heard of them. "What about you?" I ask as politely as I can. Then sit and listen patiently to his recounting of the already recycled plots of network comedies, not wanting to be perceived as snobby and aloof, not certain if I can handle so much stimulating conversation first thing in the morning.

I hurry from the office to the apartment. There is no convenient subway or bus route that would make the connection for me. I walk to and from work every day. Helps keep my legs in shape. Clears my mind of all that bothers me at home, annoys me at work. On the few days of spring when the weather is gorgeous, and the handful that occur during autumn which are sublime, my jaunts are as pleasurable as a dip in a Jacuzzi. But the frequently hot and humid days of summer, the cold and biting days of winter, predominate and make me scurry like a cockroach, leaving me tired and sweaty when it's hot, tired and itchy when cold.

To shut out the degradation of New York's streets I imagine that Lenny is walking beside me. He's dead now, but visits me sometimes. I rarely think of him at the office, but often at home. When I'm feeling lonely I conjure his face and recall the good times. Sometimes when he glides into my consciousness unbidden I cry for him. His young death. And the suffering he endured. But when I can welcome him and manage to hold onto a neutral state of mind, his visits are joyful.

He walks alongside me, keeping me company. He tells me jokes, points out the hot men, agrees with everything I say. I recall the time we drove to Jones Beach and found ourselves at the center of a flock of hungry seagulls. The beach was almost deserted that day – a bit more cloudy and cool than ideal. But we went anyway, trudged through the sand with blankets and coolers, then made camp, read books, listened to music, ate, drank beer, smoked joints. Lenny wore a fashionable baggy swimsuit, vibrant green, and I wore the traditional black Speedos. The sky, shot through with refracted sunrays, hazy, was a luminous mother-of-pearl.

I tossed a cookie to a seagull scavenging close by. The gray, sad-looking bird gobbled it, flapped its wings, and in a loud squawking vocal ejaculation, summoned about seventy relatives and close friends.

"This is like a Hitchcock film," said Lenny, as the seagulls circled closer, shrieking and flapping. He tossed them some potato chips. They became bolder, came closer, eyed our bags of goodies.

"There couldn't be any danger, could there?" I asked as goosebumps appeared on my arms and legs. I shivered.

"No danger," he said, gathering a sweatshirt around his shoulders. Then, his face taking on a lined, serious cast, asked, "Those things can't kill us, can they?"

"The water's coming closer," I said, yanking a corner of the blanket as the rising tide swallowed the sand beneath my knuckles. "Help me with the blankets."

We rose to relocate up from the water line. The birds began to scatter, but regrouped, eyeing us like hawks as soon as we were resettled. Gaining courage, they moved closer, pecking at each other, lunging like fighting cocks.

"What if they get tired of squabbling with each other and attack us?" Lenny grabbed my arm.

"I don't know," I said, feeling shivery again.

We stood up slowly. I took the bag of potato chips, tore it open and flung it as far down the beach as I could. Lenny did the same with the cookies. When the birds scattered to claim our cast-offs, we crumpled the blankets in our arms, dumped the remaining ice from the coolers, and ran, laughing – though we occasionally glanced backward – all the way back to the car.

"Shit, man," said Lenny. "Now I know how Tippi Hedren and Rod Taylor felt. Well, Tippi Hedren, anyway."

"There wasn't enough sun," I complained.

"We'll come back when it's warmer and sunnier."

"And then it'll be too crowded with suburban geeks."

"But we won't be attacked by winged monsters. All the geeks will scare them away."

My memory of the day at the beach with Lenny fades as I move around the corner to enter my building. I check the mailbox, empty, then walk up three flights and unlock the door.

Jon says, "Hi! How was your day?"

"Fine."

He pulls on his sweater. "Gotta get moving. The show must go on. I'm a Broadway Baby," he croons, smiling as though for the paparazzi.

When he's gone I begin to clean up. Return the nail clipper to the bathroom. Turn off the faucet of the kitchen sink. Replace the toothpaste tube cap. Brush the muffin crumbs off the couch and into my hand. Empty the ashtrays. Move Jon's dirty socks from the living room floor to his laundry bag. I didn't know that I'd become the janitor. The plan was to share the housework equally. I can't figure out how I allowed myself to take on such a degrading job. Why did the perfect pseudo-marriage turn into such a nightmare? This is the question I wrestle with every day.

When the apartment looks a bit less lived-in I take a shower. Finally relax. Smoke a cigarette. Eat a sandwich. If Lenny were still alive I'd call him up and complain about my job, about Jon, the apartment. But since he died I've really learned how to fill up the hours while Jon is working. I take a book from the shelf and begin to read.

It's hot, smoky, I'm standing in a bar, a place I rarely visit these days. The lights are dim. My olfactories eventually become accustomed to the odor of stale beer. Lenny or Gary, another dead friend, might sneak up behind me at any moment and whisper in my ear. Depending on their moods, they might urge me to buy a particular fellow a drink. Or they might suggest that I go home and do something constructive. Lenny might chide me for not carrying a condom. Gary could suggest that I'm drinking too much.

But I can easily dismiss them when there are so many interesting distractions. If thoughts of Lenny or Gary become too oppressive, I'll concentrate on the music from the jukebox, or the handsome junior executive-type in a three-piece suit, or the leathered bartender arguing with a customer, or the slim, younger guy looking at me with unveiled desire.

The music wraps around me like a cocoon. Alone with my thoughts, I think about the death of my sexual relationship with Jon. I can't recall at exactly which moment it died. But I can say, with certainty, that at a particular point in time we were fucking regularly and enjoying it. Then, for a while, we just went through the motions as though it were a chore of some kind. And eventually we stopped, the effort not worth the frustration. I'd begun to feel that I was doing all the work. He'd simply lie there like a corpse. I never rejected his advances. Even when I had a headache. He rejected me so often I might as well have been at a bar.

And here I am. Back in the sex market. Ironic, because the main reason I got involved with Jon was so that I could divorce myself from the dance-club-to-bar-to-sex-club circuit of fast and often unsatisfying sexual encounters. And now I'm thinking of divorcing myself from Jon. The first step being to inject myself back into the circulatory system of urban gay life.

I don't want to be here cruising, haggling like a meat merchant in a squalid, teeming marketplace. But the desire for the press of solid male flesh, the warmth of a human body, forces me to stand on the auction block, to be inspected and evaluated along with all the other prospective slaves to sensual pleasure.

A very handsome man enters, looks around, goes to the

bar and buys a bottle of imported beer. He throws his head back, his prominent Adam's apple bobbling as he swallows. He has dark hair and a trim build. Substantial thighs. I could lick those thighs until the sandpaper of my tongue removed every layer of skin. The man glances at me, I think. I smile, hoping he will approach and introduce himself. He moves closer and my heartbeat quickens. I can feel moisture on my palms. I pull back on the grin so as not to look too eager or goofy. He's so close now I can almost feel his body heat, smell his aura. As I'm about to extend my hand in greeting, he passes me and hugs another man whom, I assume, he already knows. At first I want to kill myself. Then I want to laugh. But I reveal nothing of my inner self to the strangers all around me.

It's getting late and I must remember that tomorrow is a work day. I should be asleep at a reasonable hour. But I spot a cute guy, not quite what I'm looking for – he's too thin, his face too boyish. But he looks sweet, and if I've not been misreading his glances, he's interested. I approach slowly, giving him the opportunity to look away, move elsewhere, or otherwise indicate his indifference. He remains where he is and continues to look at me.

"Hi," I say nervously, and introduce myself. We shake hands and he tells me his name. After the usual do you come here often routine, he asks what I do for a living.

"I'm a pornographer," I say, as casually as I can, as though I were a show salesman, and ask him the same question.

"Presently unemployed. Pornographer? What exactly does that mean?"

"I'm an editor. A couple of magazines."

"Like what?"

"Manmeat, Big Boys."

"Bullshit!"

"I'm not kidding," I say, trying to sound persuasive and sincere.

"You don't expect me to believe a lie like that! You think I was born yesterday? You think I'm stupid or something?"

"No, I don't think you're stupid. I'm just an ordinary guy with an unusual job, trying to have some fun."

"I've met your type before. You think that if I believe you're a big-shot editor I'll do anything you want me to do. Right?"

"Wrong."

He grunts and walks away.

I leave the bar and return home.

Jon is still at the theater. I strip, crawl into bed and try to fall asleep before he gets home.

TWO

SOMETIMES I FEEL APART FROM EVERYONE and everything. As though all the wires had been pulled, dangling in space. All the electrical impulses are motionless. Waiting for the juices to be turned on. There are no sparks at my neural endings, no activity across the tiny synapses. Although sensations can rip through my body, causing me to shudder and swoon, there is no person, no thing to receive messages. Any data or sensation directed at me does not connect. I'm in a void, walls of glass isolating me. Nothing touches me. Nothing moves me. Nor can I influence anything. Sometimes, particularly on dark rainy days, this feels good. I wallow in solitude, out of touch. But when the detachment threatens to overwhelm, I crave the other times and different feelings. When there is too much input buzzing along the wires in my brain, lights flicker, bells chime, message units jump from station to station, the volume, speed, and intensity growing to a blinding crescendo. I long to turn the switches off and melt into sleep. A dreamless slumber that offers no imagery, no mysteries, leaving nothing behind to taunt my curiosity, clutter my memory.

The telephone rings and my nerve endings start to crackle. I drop my pen and pick up the receiver. Dayna says hello. She's the only one left alive. My one living friend of any duration, the only survivor besides myself. The only person I can communicate with who won't scold or torture me. Often she uses me to unload her anger and frustration. But her complaints are rarely about my existence or behavior.

"Just thought I'd call to check in," she says. "Did you see the papers?"

I avoid the news these days. Whether printed on cheap paper or broadcast on polluted airwaves, it usually makes me sad.

"Not really. What happened?"

"The city hired a new Health Commissioner. He comes from somewhere in the Midwest. He imposed a quarantine for anyone who tests positive. If he tries it here we'll have his ass in a sling."

I don't want to talk about health issues. Mortality is easier to handle if you don't think about it.

"He'll never get away with it here," I say.

"That's what the Jews said about Hitler."

"What do you want me to do? March with a sign? Lie down in the street? Write a letter to the *Times*?"

"Just be aware of it."

"Thanks to you I am."

The curtness of her tone gives way to a voice of gentle solicitude. "How are you?" she asks.

"Well, I feel dizzy all the time and I want to throw up every fifteen minutes, but aside from that, I'm fine."

"Is there anything wrong?" she gasps.

"No. Not really. Just depressed."

"About what?"

"Aside from the job I hate, the apartment I hate, the world that's falling apart, and the fact that most of my friends are dead, I guess Jon mostly. I don't know how much longer I can take it. We barely tolerate each other. He's such a slob and I'm such a pushover. I've got to do something."

"Don't do anything rash."

"I want to break up. End this farce. He must be as miserable about our situation as I am."

"Why doesn't he move out?"

"Are you kidding?" I snicker. "While he has me to make sure the bills get paid on time, to shop for the groceries, to pick up his dirty socks? He's got it too good. I make everything too easy for him. But I also give him a hard time about it. I do everything and I wind up playing the teacher scolding the pupil. I hate it. He probably does, too."

"It's up to you to tell him you want out. If that's what you really want. Any hope for a reconciliation?"

"Not much, I think. But who knows?"

Dayna and I have had this conversation before. I'm grateful that she doesn't point this out.

"Maybe everything will work out," she says. "But if you're unhappy and don't attempt to communicate to solve the problem, then it's your fault for not being honest and open."

"I don't have the nerve or the guts. I'm too afraid of what I'll hear." I don't want to prolong this particular topic of conversation, and Dayna gets the hint when I abruptly ask how she is doing.

"Fine. Nothing happening, really."

"How's work, how's your mother, how's Martine?"

"I don't want to talk about any of that stuff. Really. I just called to hear your voice and take a break from the painting."

"What color?"

"Off-white. Kind of like eggshell."

"Which room?"

"The kitchen. After that, the bathroom and I'm done."

We exchange some meaningless chatter and the call is over.

Dayna is my rock. My anchor. Keeping me together as I verge on falling apart. Now that Lenny and Gary are gone, now that Jon and I are as compatible as oil and water, sometimes I feel like this must be hell. And then I remember Dayna, and I call her. When the conversation is over I feel a little more solid, less likely to dissipate like mist, to break down teary-eyed and sobbing.

I try to decide if I should open a book, play a CD, or turn on the television. I need to relax after another day at the office.

And then I hear Gary's voice inside my head.

Write it down, he says. Write it all down.

The voice is faint yet unmistakable. As though communicated via tin cans and waxed string. I listen and feel a tightening in my chest. I breathe deeply, and my mind slips away from the presence of Gary's voice. I swim backwards in time toward the moment I first met him.

In a living room. Someone's apartment. I can't recall whose home it was. Sitting in various postures on the chairs and sofas encircling a coffee table were eight men. The youngest, I believe, was Gary, about twenty-seven at the time. The oldest, probably Joe, in his mid-forties. All styles of dress and hair. All of us white and gay. All of us determined to become writers. This was the first meeting of what became a workshop which met periodically for almost five years. Of course, eventually, some people quit. Others joined. Some died.

But on that first night, I could not have predicted that the group would have any longevity. And I did not know that I would become a longterm participant. I was vibrating with excitement and information came at me too rapidly. I couldn't absorb everything. Finally, I was doing something about which I'd only dreamed. To try to learn writing skills, to find a voice, to tell stories which might move someone to chuckles, pangs, or shivers.

And for the first time I was among people who were active readers. Many of us had actually read some of the same books. This was a new experience for me. Most of my friends and acquaintances never read anything. Except for headlines, comics, TV listings, and sports scores in the newspapers. And I, who'd been devouring fiction and poetry ever since I learned to read, was starved for companions who could share the pleasures of the text.

Gary was handsome and sexy. Blond hair, warm blue eyes, a trim physique, he moved with athletic grace. But the first night I hardly noticed his appearance. I was too impressed by his mention of a book I'd just finished. And it amazed me when several others had something to say about this particular book as well. I felt like I'd been imprisoned on a deserted asteroid, doomed to float through silence and darkness. And then, unexpectedly, a star imploded, illuminating my surroundings, freeing me from my drifting cage, delivering me to a lush garden populated with beings of my own devising.

Once I'd become accustomed to this luxury, these meetings that occurred every two weeks, I was able to transcend the limitations of my initial excitement and begin to examine the particularities of the group's members. All were affable. Some more serious and experienced than others. A uniformly high intelligence level became apparent. I liked everyone. Did not feel a special affinity for one or another.

Until one night when Gary placed a book in my hands and said that I might like it. As time receded and approached, we'd comment on each other's short stories, all the while exchanging books. We'd talk about them. Agree occasionally. And soon began to spend time together on nights when there was no meeting to attend. Eventually we'd meet for dinner, plays, movies. But we always talked about books and writing, reading and literature, style and content.

I finally had a friend whom I didn't have to deceive, pretend that I was more interested than I really was. Act like I was enjoying myself while boredom overwhelmed me. Gary stripped me of pretense and artifice.

When we were together I felt fulfilled. Food, sex, sleep, money could not compete with the hours we spent. I allowed myself to imagine that Gary and I might still be friends when we became stooped, toothless, and bald.

It's been about three years since he died. And his visitations are not like they were when his lungs still breathed and his heart still kept time.

I look up from my pad, and my consciousness returns to the apartment. Glancing around, I see nobody there, although I could swear Gary had just been there. I put down the pen. Aloud, to the emptiness, I say, "I'm writing it all down, Gary. Are you listening? Can you hear me? I'm writing it all down."

* * *

Telephones ring, the freight elevator rumbles and rattles. Several radios tuned to different stations create a jarring fugue. I'm too busy to think about anything which might bring a sliver of pleasure. There's too much to consider, I'm too preoccupied to notice.

Stacks of things surround me. Stacks that I must sift and evaluate. There are color slides lined up right to left and top to bottom in clear plastic sleeves. Manila envelopes contain short stories. Slips of paper from the receptionist with phone numbers, names, times, dates, and reminders. Notes on yellow stick-'em flags so I won't forget anything important.

The slides are miniature photographs of naked men. Most have muscular bodies. A few are handsome. All have big, erect dicks.

The short stories are, for the most part, poorly written and fall easily into such categories as sailor, cowboy, cop, student, beach, forest, cabin, apartment, suburban, foreign, past and future.

I can read two stories in succession, but then must rest my eyes. So I look at several sets of slides and that bores me. My brain, like a thick soup, is a swirl of fragments and muted pigments. Few of the pictures or stories manage to stir the juices of my scrotum. I wonder if the pages of the magazines will arouse anyone at all.

I've been at the office for less than two hours and already I wish I could go home.

Even though Jon's there.

I throw my head back and breathe deeply. Then light a cigarette and look at the phone messages. My extension chimes shrilly and I lift the receiver with apprehension. Who will it be? Jon? Dayna? Mother? The boss? A disgruntled writer? A dissatisfied subscriber? An angry photographer? A frustrated illustrator? A bewildered model? A puzzled reader? A pushy advertiser? A harried printer? A brusque distributor? A rude competitor? A nasty evangelist?

"Yes," I say, expectant.

"Um, um, um."

"Hello? Anybody there? Can I help you?"

"Is this, um, is this, um?"

This guy needs all the help he can get. "To whom do you wish to speak?"

"Um, the editor."

"The editor of which magazine?" I ask, considering the possibility that he's not calling about *Manmeat* or *Big Boys,* but *Dairy Queens* or *Bad Girls.*

"Um, um," his voice lowers into a breathy whisper, *"Manmeat."*

Now we're finally getting somewhere. "I'm the editor of *Manmeat,* what can I do for you?"

After several halting sounds, snorts, and other verbal ejaculations that do not mean anything in English, he finally spurts, in that same breathy whisper, "I want to be a model."

The phrase strikes my fearful heart like a poisoned spear. Most people who phone a porn editor and express an interest in removing their clothing for a camera are off to a bad start. Like a writer who sends manuscripts to a big-time agent, like a rock group that sends a demo tape to a large record company, the chances of anything good happening are remote. If they come to you, something might happen. When you go to them, forget it.

"Send me a picture," I say.

"A picture?" he says in disbelief, as though this obvious necessity has not occurred to him, which it probably hasn't, because in my experience, people who want to become porn models usually lack the brain power of a doorknob.

"Yes, a picture, a photograph, nude. One in which I can clearly see your face, body, and genitals. If you can, a rear-view shot would be helpful too."

There is a long pause during which he is presumably thinking about this.

In most cases, a man who winds up stark naked, hard-dicked, bent and spread in a magazine, gets there because he has been spotted somewhere by a professional photographer. In extremely rare cases, a call followed by a photo might work. But a point-of-contact situation is the norm. Walking down the street, standing in a bar, pumping at the gym, lounging in the dunes, are more likely avenues toward appearing in a magazine or video.

"A picture?" he asks again.

"Yes," I reaffirm.

"Can't I just come up to the office and, you know, you know, um."

"Take your clothes off and show me what you've got?"

"Yeah, that's it."

I immediately think of the incident which is the reason why I will never again see a potential model off the street. Not since my encounter with The Entrepreneur and The Kid. I hadn't been a pornographer for very long, and when I was hired I knew almost nothing about the field. Familiar with correct English usage and a knowledge of modern and post-modern fiction, I became the editor of a magazine which specializes in photography. The joke is on me. My mentor, Jonah, taught me everything as we went along. He supplied me with insider information such as which gay porn stars aren't really gay and other useful tidbits. When I asked him, "If they're not really gay, how can they have sex with other men?"

"It's for the camera," he said.

"But they're still having sex."

"And they're being paid."

"True."

"Sometimes," he said, with the professional hush that means you should listen closely and be discreet, "the stars of the film just do the preliminary stuff. Then when you see the close-ups of dicks and asses with penetration and every-thing, they use a stand-in."

"Ah-hah!" I said, feeling as though I'd just joined an exclu-sive club and learned its best-kept secret.

One day Jonah told me that someone was coming to the office, a potential model, and asked if I'd like to attend the audition. We went to the conference room at the appointed hour and waited. Although the work space is cheap and cluttered, the conference room, spacious and elegant, was designed to impress and lure clients. We sat in the fancy leather and chrome chairs, smoking cigarettes. A few minutes later a middle-aged man, The Entrepreneur, and a kid, The Kid, came in. We all shook hands. The Entrepreneur produced papers proving The Kid was nineteen years old. He looked his age, but he seemed to be less than average, as far as his sex appeal quotient goes. His face looked tortured, as though pressed against a windowpane. Cross-eyed and drooling, he did not conform to my conception of sexy. He had a hard and tight teenager's body, but so do many kids. Few, though, are porn star material. It was obvious right away that The Kid's brain was on a permanent vacation, and that The Entrepreneur was smothering him like a bell jar over a candle. Jonah addressed The Kid and asked him why he wanted to be in porn magazines. He burbled something, dribbled, stammered, and finally looked to The Entrepreneur for help. "This is a financial arrangement," he said, like P. T. Barnum, I thought. "The kid has talent – you should see him naked – and I'm his manager." I glanced at Jonah, an uneasy feeling in my stomach. I wondered if I'd get to see The Kid's dick, if this meeting might erupt into a full-scale orgy. Jonah looked at me. He silently acknowledged that he could not delude these two into thinking that there was any chance for The Kid ever to amount to anything in magazines and videos. He wasn't very handsome and he didn't seem very willing.

Jonah asked, "Do you like to take your clothes off when people are watching?"

The Kid trembled and looked at The Entrepreneur.

"There's no problem with that! You should see what the kid's got between his legs."

Jonah ignored him and looked at The Kid. "Are you aware of how little money there is in this? Models don't get rich. Publishers and producers make all the money. Even if you manage to get your photographs into every men's magazine this year and also appear in half a dozen videos, you'll still be earning sub-poverty wages."

The Entrepreneur huffed incredulously. He suspected Jonah of lying.

"It's true," Jonah said. "Everyone thinks these guys make a lot of money – and they do – peddling their ass to smelly old men seven nights a week. The money they earn from the magazines and the videos barely pays for lube and condoms."

Too greedy to accept the truth, The Entrepreneur said, "Let us show you what we're selling here."

He instructed his client to stand up and strip. The Kid cringed and began to cry. "Right here? Now?" he stammered.

I felt very uncomfortable and wanted to throw up. By this time I had no desire to see his dick.

"Remember!" shouted The Entrepreneur, "I told you you'd have to do this!"

"No!" wailed the kid. He shot to his feet and headed for the door. Flinging it open, he ran down the hall to the elevator. While The Entrepreneur apologized for his client's unprofessional behavior, The Kid entered the elevator and disappeared. The Entrepreneur assured us he'd send some slides.

When The Entrepreneur left, I wondered if the kid was waiting for him in the lobby, or if he'd run away. I had several nightmares about this incident. Undereducated, lacking street smarts, and not too bright, The Kid would have to rely on older, wiser people, some of whom would take advantage.

Several months later Jonah received a packet of slides. The Kid, naked, looking uncomfortable and scared. Not one single shot of an erection. The kid was probably too shy. Perhaps even terrified. You have to be an exhibitionist to have any success in porn. You must have ample equipment and be eager to show it off. The Entrepreneur and The Kid were fooling themselves. I shudder when I think of them and what they might be up to now.

This memory, like a splinter in my brain, is too sharp to ignore or forget. Breathing deeply, I return to the caller, the porn-star wannabe who thinks he'll impress me in person, and slowly inform him that it's against company policy for anyone to remove his or her clothing on the premises. "You must send a photo," I reiterate. "If I think you have potential, I'll forward it to a photographer."

"But I ain't got no pictures."

"What else can I tell you, get some made."

"Shit, man."

This guy is probably a crackhead and needs fast money for a fix, I tell myself.

"Can't I just come over, I'm just a few blocks away, and show you what I've got?"

"Sorry." Maybe he thinks there are naked hunks roaming the corridors, snorting coke, sipping margaritas, dancing to disco music, and he just wants to party. "I have deadlines to meet, I'm under the tyranny of the clock, and I don't have any more time for this. If you can't send a photo you're out of luck. Have a nice day."

I hang up, glance out the window. Everything is blurry. It feels like my head's been split open and my brains have spilled out onto the floor. I must shovel the mess back into the empty skull where it belongs. I massage my forehead and walk to the water cooler to clear my mind. As I sip the cool wetness, someone from the accounting department asks if I watched *That's Life* last night. When I tell her no, she insists on relating all the details and one-liners which I've already been told more than once.

Up the worn slanting steps that can kill you if you're not careful, past the dusty pockmarked walls painted tan trimmed in red, beneath chipping, falling plaster, I trudge three flights, passing the scents of marijuana, cat, boiling cabbage, incense. Key in the lock, twist hard, jiggle, twist hard, shoulder to wood, door opens.

Sit-ups, push-ups, a shower, and a snack are what I crave, but first I must clean up after Jon. There is the mug of cold coffee on the table that has to go into the sink, and the ring left on the table to remove. I turn off the still-running cold water tap in the bathroom, twist the cap of the toothpaste tube back into place. The television flickers silently, the lights of the VCR glow in the late afternoon light. I turn them off and I empty the ashtrays. A cigarette, burned to the filter, on top of the stove gets flicked into the trash can.

The hot water on my flesh feels like a massage. My pulse slows, the tension in my forehead slips away. I soap myself, angle my body to catch the cascades, and feel the muscles in my shoulders and back relax. Breathing hot steam, washing the office from my body and my mind, my thoughts turn to Jon and the time when I loved him.

For my birthday Jon bought me a five-gallon aquarium and a Siamese fighting fish, the most beautiful male betta I'd ever seen. Long, flowing fins, a deep blue shot through with streaks of flaming burgundy, a hint of green iridescence fanning through the tail. Max, as we called him, would swim haltingly, surveying every angle, flourishing his gaudy fins like a drag queen.

I'd always wanted to breed bettas, having tried and failed while fulfilling a high school science requirement. The week after Jon bought Max, I went shopping for a mate. Missy, we called her, a scarlet temptress, and hoped that she would find Max to be a suitable companion and vice versa.

Many aquarium fish couple and reproduce automatically. Others find captivity too unsexy. But bettas can be bred in tanks if the keepers follow a few simple rules. The fish, as well, observe a routine, an intricate ritual, actually. The male builds a nest, blowing bubbles on the surface of the water. These are held together by a viscous secretion in his mouth. When the nest is completed and the female is thick with eggs, they are brought together after a few days of separation with a transparent divider, and begin courting.

Missy seeks out Max and attempts a snuggle. He responds by nipping at her and chasing her all over the tank. She finds refuge in the dense plants and eventually seeks his company again. This part of the dating phase can go on for some time, with the female getting slightly shredded and roughed up in the process. One theory holds that the male is testing the female to see if she has the stamina to endure the rigors of reproduction. If he does not deem her hardy enough, he supposedly loses interest. Max and Missy's mutual attraction did not sag for a moment. But the chase went on for days. Jon and I thought they'd never get to the X-rated part.

Whenever Jon and I were together during the breeding of the bettas, we had plenty to talk about. Did we think Missy was getting too frayed? Are the temperature and pH level correct? Are we feeding them enough? What are we going to do with all the babies? We had long conversations that lasted until sunrise. It's possible that we were never as close and intimate as those weeks and months of surrogate parenthood, as we gathered our hopes together, instinctively perhaps, for young and innocent beings whom we could nurture, raise, and feel responsible for.

When they finally tired of their crazed chases, Max and Missy met beneath the bubble nest. She went into a trance and floated, unmoving and corpse-like, in the still water. He wrapped his body around her, squeezing a profusion of eggs from her ovipositor. Then, she came back to life and both of them gathered the tiny white eggs in their mouths and blew them up into the bubblecluster. They repeated this action more times than we felt like counting.

Jon and I knew, from the manuals we'd read, that when they were done it was time to move Missy to another tank, which we'd been prepared for, Jon having decided to acquire another. Once the eggs are laid and ensconced, the father becomes super-overprotective and attacks any other fish – including the mommy – who dares to come too close.

It takes about forty-eight hours for the eggs to hatch. During this time Max kept rebuilding the nest as it broke apart, catching the falling eggs. When the tiny babies began to appear, he'd herd them back to the nest when they strayed too far away. Some of the infants grew rapidly, others remained small for a long time. When they became free-swimmers and started to eat the baby food we gave them, Max was removed to another tank.

My relationship with Jon shrank back to where it had floundered prior to our acquisition of the bettas. Only a temporary dam to hold back the waters of discontent. When Max and Missy's children became independent, so did we.

THREE

DAD, I MISS YOU. WHY DID YOU LEAVE ME? How could you do this to Mom? Dad, I love you and wish I'd said it more often. I see your face, but I don't know if you can hear me. Ours is a history of bad connections. Dad, I think I'm dying. There's something wrong with me. I have a funny taste in mouth, my feet feel numb, my energy level is low. I'm not sure what it is but I fear the worst. I want you to make it all right. You were the master of all things when I was a small boy. Your simplest gestures moved me like earthquakes. A cigar box that you gave me when it was finally empty became my whole world. The box smelled sweet, opening and closing majestically. And the illustration on top and gold trim all around impressed my innocent eyes. The intricacy of the lines, like a peppery filigree, the translucent blue, the stately red, the royal gold, the fine cut of the gentlemen's period clothing. I can't recall the brand, nor can I describe the subject of the illustration. But the colors, contours, lines, shapes, and arabesques are like slides I can drop into a projector. And the aroma. Breathing deeply, it's here now, with me in this room.

I want to know what you're afraid of. Maybe then I can tell you my fears. Our only moment of pure communication was never completed. A fragment of truth jumped the gap between us. We almost resolved all the tension. But the fragment lacked the wholeness that could have made a difference. Perhaps, if you'd lived longer, we'd have come closer at another time.

The failed messages, the undelivered notes are like spiky shards in my memory. Like shackles on bruised ankles, they keep me in step. Reminders of all the flaws, mistakes, imperfections of my life.

When my friend Dan and I were seniors in high school he'd sleep over sometimes, remember? Usually it was on a night when you and Mom were going to come home very late. He and I would sleep in the double bed in the attic. To me it was always an adventure to sleep away from my room. But this night I got more than I planned for.

As soon as you and Mom left and we heard the garage door closing, Dan and I each took a tab of acid. Years later, I told you that I'd tripped more than a few times. But that night, you knew nothing of my drug experiences. I don't recall what kind of evening you and Mom had. Whether you went to a theater, or a party or a business function. But while you were gone, Dan and I saw the world beneath our skin, beyond our eyes. The walls and ceilings spoke to us, record covers came to life and danced joyously to music we'd heard a million times but had never listened to before. I felt supercharged and tingly, my skin like hot velvet, heart like a nuclear reactor, my brain a huge switchboard with tendrils reaching out to the stars. We laughed and cried, talked about how large and small we'd become. Drank a sip of wine which tasted like the tears of a sad and beautiful angel.

Eventually you and Mom returned. Dan and I did our best to act like everything was normal. Of course, I felt like I would explode at any moment, but I pretended to be sane. You looked like a creature from outer space. Mom appeared to me like a red-haired ocelot, sleek and graceful.

"We're going to watch some TV for a while," I announced as you and Mom got ready for bed. Dan and I drank tea all night and stared at a test pattern when the station signed off. We sat on the floor, smoking one cigarette after another, studying the black and white lines, the tiny pixels that entered our brains like lances. When you awakened at your usual time, around 6:30, I think, you heard us giggling in the living room. You walked in, tying your bathrobe, your dark hair in lopsided swirls around your face. You glanced at the TV set, then down at Dan and me on the floor, the ashtray between us.

"Are you boys trying to kill yourselves?" you spat bitterly, then walked out and got ready for work. Dan and I sobered up very quickly.

"How did he know we took acid?" Dan asked, astonished.

"I don't know," I said. "Maybe we were acting so weird he could just tell."

I became frightened. Would you throw me out? What would the punishment be?

Dan and I cut school that day. We sat in the coffee shop near the train station, dizzy from the lack of sleep and the afterglow of the acid, wondering if you would call his parents. Tell them your son and my son are drug addicts. We agonized all day long, afraid to go home. But finally, we had no choice.

That evening, sitting at the dinner table, Mom remarked that I looked tired. I was waiting for you to scold me about drugs. You looked at Mom and said, "Between the two of them our son and Dan smoked an entire pack of cigarettes and never went to bed. They watched television all night long."

Mom told me how disappointed she was. You fixed me with a cold stare and said, "If you want to kill yourself, don't do it while I'm still alive."

Nothing you've ever said terrified me more. The concept of you being dead was something I simply couldn't grasp. I thought you'd never leave me. But I sat there, stunned, because for the first time ever, I was forced to take death seriously.

At the same time that I was contemplating the harsh realities of mortality, I was elated that you hadn't mentioned drugs. In fact, you didn't know that we'd been tripping our brains out. I'd been terrified all day for the wrong reason. Smoking cigarettes and staying up all night was what had upset you. Part of me wanted to laugh. But I also wanted to cry. I felt stomach-sick. I couldn't eat anything. I'd read you all wrong, and someday you would die. I was not prepared for it then and I'm still not now.

I may be dying. Of, you know, *it.* It's so difficult to say. Because by voicing the sound, maybe you allow it to come closer. If you dare to speak it, then it can touch you. Infect you. To remain silent is to deny it. I feel like a superstitious aborigine who believes that he can bring rain by climbing into the highest branches of the tallest tree and pouring water from a gourd.

Dad, I love you. And I hated seeing you sick. All the tubes and wires and medication. The look on your face. Pain. I couldn't stand to see you like that. You were so kind and generous. Everyone loved you. You never harmed anyone. Why did you have to suffer so?

When I visited Lenny in the hospital, about a week before he died, I felt exactly the same as when I saw you in the hospital. Helpless. And alone. Frightened that this is surely my destiny as well. When you died, Dad, you were in your seventies. Lenny was only thirty-three, Gary, thirty-five. I'm thirty-eight now and I doubt I'll see forty. I'll never see Paris or Florence or Barcelona – even if I manage to live. I have no money. Not like you had. I work as hard as you did. I'm as exhausted every night as you were when you would drive in bumper-to-bumper traffic for two hours every evening on the Long Island Expressway, sit through dinner arguing and fighting with Greg and me. Then you'd lie on the couch, ostensibly to watch TV. And you'd be snoring before the first commercial.

I remember the shouting contests between you and Greg and me at dinner. Mom was the mediator. But then when I went away to college, relations improved. Didn't they? You and I became better friends. Didn't we? We still had our differences. We still argued. But the disputes were quieter, friendlier. Yes? I guess we just couldn't live together. It's probably me. I can't seem to live with Jon either.

You were always so accepting. Like when I came out to you and Mom and we went to see *Making Love.* Do you remember that movie? About the guy who leaves his wife for another guy? Kate Jackson. You always liked her. You liked all of *Charlie's Angels.* But I remember how good it felt when you and Mom and I went to see the movie. I sat between the two of you, gauging your reactions. We'd fought over the tickets. Up until that time you'd paid for everything including the popcorn and sodas whenever we'd been to a theater together. I insisted on buying those tickets. You said it was out of the question. Mom intervened.

"Let him buy the tickets if he wants to, dammit!"

You looked at her, mumbled something. And gave in.

Sitting there nervously, wondering how you and everyone else in the audience would respond, I entered a state of acute anticipation. Some might call it an anxiety attack. I feared that the sight of two adult men kissing and rolling around on a bed might be too much. You and Mom had come to terms with my sexuality, so you said, but I wondered if you could handle the reality of male flesh on male flesh. As Harry Hamlin brought his lips to Michael Ontkean's I felt an electric current pass through my soul. Straining my peripheral vision, trying not to turn my head, I looked right and left to see how you and Mom were responding. Both of you were blank spaces to be filled in by my paranoia. You could have been watching a cat food commercial, so unreadable were your faces. No one in the audience threw popcorn at the screen. I could detect no derisive reactions. Walking through the floodlit parking lot toward the car I asked how you liked it.

"Very good," said Mom.

"It was like a television movie," you said, "only better."

"That Michael Ontkean is very handsome," said Mom, both of you always commenting on the appearances of TV and movie stars.

You shook your head. "No, the other one, Harry something, he's better looking."

Both of you looked at me.

"I wouldn't kick either one out of bed," I said, holding my breath.

You chuckled. Then threw back your head and laughed. Mom giggled. I relaxed like a coil spring stretched to the limit for twenty-six years.

I'm one of the lucky ones, Dad. When I told you about my secret life, when I revealed that I was editing porn magazines, you didn't turn your back on me. You didn't lecture me or express any disapproval. Some parents never talk to their children again. Feuds have erupted, lives have been ruined, dynasties have been shattered by the mere utterance: I'm gay. These words, which could have separated us forever, brought us closer. You hugged me and kissed me, told me I'd always be your son. I'd prepared myself for the possibility that I might never see you again. That you might hate me forever. But you saved me from myself. Something you did often. And I feel empty at times, thinking that I never gave you half as much as you gave me. I only knew how to take. But I think I've grown and learned a few things. If you were here with me now, maybe I could make up for my youthful foolishness. I would be more attentive, more considerate, less contrary if we were together today. I think I could show you that I've learned to be a giver and I'm not just a taker like before. There is nothing I wouldn't do to earn your respect, make you sizzle with pride. But it's too late now. I said the wrong things and made many mistakes. It's impossible to erase that past and there's no way to compensate in the future. I feel that I have failed you. But if I had the chance, I'd do it better the next time.

Are you listening?

I know you would have liked it better if I'd become a doctor, lawyer, or some other kind of person with money. You always knew I was somewhat rebellious. That I'd never follow the easiest path, the expected route, do the traditional thing. But you know what's really ironic about my life? I sold out and don't even have the money to show for it. When I saw how you were tortured five days a week, could perceive the weakening of your spirit, I swore I'd never work a nine-to-five job. I'd be a musician or a writer. I'd never be a superstar, far too eccentric and unyielding for that, but I'd earn a living apart from the establishment and its bureaucracies. I found out it's very difficult. The chances for making it big are few, there is no middle ground. You become rich and famous or you starve and struggle. If you try to be innovative or original, you are shunned like leper. After going through the music wringer, I worked in an off-Broadway box office for a while, then I finally took a grueling job in publishing, thinking that because porn sells so well I'd make some bucks. But the only one getting rich is my boss. And it destroys me that I put out so much to make his magazines succeed and he pays me a janitor's salary. But that's not my only financial problem. There's the government's defense budget which chomps huge clumps of my meager earnings, and the IRS clobbers me every April because I'm not married and don't have any children. Then there's the taxes on my freelance work: the government punishes me for writing in my spare time when I should be eating pretzels, swilling beer, and watching television. I work so hard and I have no money. By the time you were my age you could afford a house, two cars, and vacations in Europe. I live on tuna fish, peanut butter, and for me to spend a weekend in Philadelphia I'd have to skip lunch and save like a miser for about five years.

You always measured everything in money. I knew you could appreciate other things. But I feel that I would have pleased you more if I'd become wealthy. There are a few things I'm proud of, though. I've never raped, murdered or stolen. I help old ladies across the street and never litter. I'm honest and reliable. I try to keep educating myself. I fight for the rights of humans, animals, and the planet. I work hard, pay my bills on time, and vote. Does any of this matter to anyone? Or is it just the size of my bank account?

I know that we came from different backgrounds. You grew up in a poor family, and therefore developed a respect for money. You gave me a childhood of affluence and I took money for granted. But perhaps there's something else. Maybe there's a component inside me that ignores the craving for money because I will never have the responsibilities of a husband or father. Could your ambition have been spurred by the need to be a good provider for your eventual family?

There's another thing, too. Although you encouraged me to be studious and knowledgeable, you were always anti-intellectual. You preferred easy entertainment to challenging art, a silly television program to a serious film. You never read anything but spy thrillers, always chose a weightless musical over a heavy drama. Yet you wanted me to study Shakespeare and Beethoven, to know about the great philosophers and scientists. I became what you wanted me to be. Except that I exist on the poverty line.

I don't feel at home in this world. Society as we know it is not comfortable with me. I'm too different. Not standard issue. My ideas about everything, like sex, art, and money, are at odds with the majority.

You were always so stylish and acceptable. I dressed for comfort, didn't care what anyone thought, and hated the pretensions of fashion slaves. We fought over my wardrobe all the time. I'd want sneakers, you wanted me to wear wing tips. I wanted jeans, you insisted on gray flannel. I hated, and still do, suits, ties, cufflinks, tie clasps. You had the world's largest collection and expected me to follow your lead. And I didn't care if your hair was too long or not perfectly styled. Do you remember the fight we had right before I left for college?

It was just two days prior to registration. You and Mom would drive me to Boston. A haircut was mandatory, you said. I'd planned on growing my hair long. This was the early seventies. Lots of men had long, flowing hair. That's what I wanted. You, however, insisted that I have a standard cut.

I rebelled.

Mom said, "What will people think? Going around looking like a slob! Is that the way we raised you?" Her eyes became moist and her face froze in disappointment.

"When are you going to grow up and develop a sense of responsibility?" you said.

I wasn't trying to displease you. Simply trying to assert my selfhood, my desire for freedom and autonomy. But you and Mom could aim guilt arrows right to the bull's-eye of my conscience. Nothing could shield me from your disapproval.

You and I did not speak to each other for a while. Mom was the conciliator. I sat on my bed staring at the wall, anxious about leaving for college, upset that you and I were not talking. Mom sat beside me and told me that a friend of hers knew of a unisex boutique in Manhattan that styled men's hair. Would I prefer this to the usual barber shop shredding? The thought of having my hair styled did not appeal. But I was eager to make up with you and I was curious to see what a unisex boutique was all about. Mom made an appointment for me.

I drove into the city the next morning, excited because, at the time, I loved driving in Manhattan. The boutique was on the third floor of a small building on Second Avenue. The women who worked there were skinny and very fashionable. The men were all flamboyantly gay. Richie cut my hair. He asked what I wanted and I told him I had no idea, whatever he thought would be best. He had very short hair, big eyes and a tiny waist. When he touched my hair I felt goosebumpy. This man had presumably had sex with other men and he was touching me. I guess I got a little excited. Richie was cute. And he did a nice job on my hair. The layered look, or a shag cut, as it was called. But I hated it. It made me look like the terribly unhip corporate cog I've always striven to avoid becoming. I thanked Richie, tipped him, and gave his hand a lingering shake.

Driving back home, I thought at least you would be pleased even though I was not.

At dinner that night we sat in silence. I waited for some comment from you and Mom. The quiet became overwhelming. "Are you happy?" I asked, the sarcasm dripping from my mouth like lemon juice.

"Very nice," said Mom.

"Very nice," you concurred.

I slammed down my salad fork.

"Well, I hate it!"

You looked at me with a pained grin and admitted, "I hate it, too."

I became a bullet struck by a firing pin. The veins in my wrists stood out like coaxial cables, my face locked in a scowl. I picked up the plate I was eating from, smashed it to the floor and ran from the table. You and Mom sat there, stunned. Greg just kept eating, grateful, I suppose, that this particular conflict did not involve him. I went to the drawer by the telephone and seized the scissors. Slashing away at my hair, I began to cry, shuddering and moaning, hot tears streaking my face. You ran to me and tried to take the scissors. I cut my finger. When the sharp metal pierced my skin and I saw the bubble of bright red, I threw the scissors to the floor and ran out of the house.

Hours later, when I'd been sitting in the backyard, the air chilly, you brought me a jacket. Told me to come inside. Then bandaged my finger. I looked in the mirror. My hair didn't look as bad as I thought it would after I'd hacked away at it.

"It'll grow in soon," I said.

You kissed me. Apologized for cutting my finger.

I let you take the blame, Dad. In all the years when I could have confessed the truth, I let you think that it was you who'd manipulated the scissors. But it was me. I didn't do it intentionally. It was accidental. But it wasn't your fault! It was my clumsiness. In my anger I lost control. Even if you hadn't been trying to take the scissors from me, my frenzied slashing would have resulted in a wound of some sort. Perhaps you saved me from cutting my face, my ears, my neck.

I'm so sorry to have deceived you.

I wish I'd told you this before you died.

I hope that you can hear me.

FOUR

FOR A WHILE I FELT DETACHED from the viral mania. As my friends began to sicken and die, as the stories and rumors became more horrifying, I encysted myself, attempting to escape the harsh realities. But the slimy, clawed tentacles of the disease can penetrate the most formidable suits of armor and maximum security enclosures. No one is really safe. But for brief periods you can trick yourself into thinking you're immune. There were times when I felt like an entertainer on a Bob Hope Christmas Special, dropped in to amuse the troops, lifted out and flown to safety. But now I'm a soldier, stuck in the fetid jungle, napalm devouring the trees and shrubs. At any moment the creeping ooze will reach my feet and I'll begin to dissolve.

It started with a trip to the dentist for my usual gum-scraping. With the scent of mouthwash in the air and the sound of whirring drills like flies about my ears, I sat in the space-age chair beside the green robot, waiting for the treatment to begin. The dentist examined my open mouth, shook his head and sighed. Then informed me that he wouldn't treat me until I'd seen a doctor and shown him the inside of my mouth.

"Why?" I asked, almost knowing that something was terribly wrong.

"You have a fungus and I can't work on your teeth until it's cleared up."

I made an appointment with a doctor. His office smelled like disinfectant. He looked inside my mouth and told me to move my tongue around. Gathering his facial features into an advertisement for doom, he stared at me and solemnly delivered the death sentence. "Thrush, a sign of immunosuppression. You should take the test and start medication right away, if necessary."

I didn't want to deal with the weight of AIDS just then.

I simply wanted my teeth cleaned.

"Doctor, I don't want to take the test. I'm scared enough as it is. Besides, I can't afford all those expensive medications."

"Do you have a health plan at work?"

"Yes."

"Then don't worry about the cost. Think about trying to stay alive until a cure is found. You have to face the facts."

I saw myself, lesioned and skeletal, rotting in a buried coffin.

"All right," I said, and rolled up my sleeve.

He filled a syringe with my blood. I couldn't watch. I stared at the soft green wall. My brain felt like a punching bag. The test was unnecessary. The alien creature living inside my mouth told the entire story. In seconds my status had changed from upper-caste to untouchable.

I felt like I'd been tortured with electric cattle prods as I walked home from the doctor's office. There were few pedestrians to distract me. It seemed to take forever.

I trudged up the stairs of the building with heavy chains of death clanking, weighing me down. Entering the apartment was like facing a firing squad. I undressed to take a cold shower. Standing on worn porcelain, I turned the faucet knob. It gurgled, produced seven drops of water, then hissed and stopped. I checked the hot water faucet. Nothing.

Moments later, a fist pounded my door. I wrapped myself in a bathrobe. "Who's there?"

"Frank."

The accountant who lives two floors below.

I opened the door. His face, usually bright and attractive looked sunken and forbidding. "The bitch turned off the water again."

"I know. I just found out."

"Mind if I come in?"

He sat on the couch, right next to the aquarium, as I closed the door.

"What are we gonna do?" he moaned, then intertwined his fingers and hugged his knees with his forearms. "I can't take any more of this shit! I pay my rent on time and half the time I need water it's turned off!"

"Not half the time," I say, gently, to try to calm him down.

"Often enough!" he spat. His face became redder, the lines in his forehead deepened. "We've tried everything and nothing seems to work. Sometimes I just want to smack the bitch!"

"That won't solve anything," I said. "Did you call downstairs to see if they could tell you anything?"

"The bartender said nothing could be done until tomorrow."

"Shit," I said.

"Yeah," he agreed.

Frank left. I was torn between fretting about the plumbing in my building and the pipes and valves of my body. Jon arrived home a short while later.

"Hi," he said, tentatively. He looked so sweet and innocent in his running shorts, his hair wind-swept, his face flushed. I recalled the times when he'd kiss me when he returned home.

"Hi," I said. "Bad news – don't kill the messenger."

He slung his backpack to the floor and frowned. "What now?"

"No water."

"Fuck! Why the hell not?"

"The usual."

"The bitch that owns the restaurant downstairs?"

"Who else?"

"She has no right. Only the landlord can turn off the water. I'll bet she didn't even post a note or warn anyone either." He paced back and forth near the television set, pounding his thighs with his fists.

I lowered my voice, trying to soothe him. "The plumbing in this building is prehistoric. Whenever there's a leak into the restaurant below, she turns the building's water off. She's the only one with access to the valves."

"But it's against the law! The landlord's the only one who has the right to turn it off!"

"You know it and I know it, but she's the one with her hand on the knob."

"Why can't they just put a bucket beneath the leak?"

"Don't ask me."

"Fuck goddammit!" he yelled, then scowled at me and fixed himself a vodka and orange juice. I rolled a joint. We sat together and relaxed. I decided to wait for the right moment to tell him about the fungus in my mouth.

The times when it's just the two of us against destiny are when we're closest. We circle the wagons and try to defend our turf from the marauding attackers. If the water is off, electricity not working, no heat on fierce winter nights, we are like one entity, fighting to survive.

To escape the anguish, we talk.

I try to lighten the mood by joking, "What do you think of Red China?"

"I don't know," he replies, his sculpted face Byronic, beautiful, and sad.

"You're supposed to say, 'It depends on the color of the tablecloth.'"

"Ha, ha," he scoffed, but the mention of China got us off and running, the topic the internationalization of economics. "I can't believe what's happening. People everywhere are beginning to realize that countries are becoming obsolete and corporations are gaining the real power." His features soften after he gets this off his chest. The moodiness disappears and he looks boyishly happy, his eyes wide, lips parted.

One of the things that brought Jon and me together was our ability to talk endlessly about any number of subjects. Our primary topics are literature, film, theater, music. Politics is something to discuss when we've exhausted all the cultural possibilities. After we'd met and had our first date for dinner, I remember I was astonished to find that he was reading *Moby Dick*. It's one of my favorite books and I'd never been able to interest any of my friends in reading it. I always wanted to discuss it with someone and there was Jon. Great in bed. A good conversationalist. And he was reading *Moby Dick*.

"I'm getting the impression," he'd said, "that Melville must have been queer as a goose. Closeted maybe. Or repressed. It seems like he tried to hide his sexual inclinations, but they seep out onto every page he wrote."

I recall that the conversation loosely covered a lot of territory as we got a general impression of each other's interests. And as we got to know one another better, and began to develop a shared history, the talk reached new heights of intensity. I think I may have fallen in love with Jon after just such a conversation.

I admit I had a slight crush on Gary. In addition to his intelligence and personality, he was an aficionado of physical culture. He worked out, swam, cycled. His body was solid and beautifully outlined, his walk, posture, stance all suggested an athletic armature revved up and bursting with energy. Every motion displayed the smooth workings of a finely-tuned musculature. I sensed what waited beneath his clothing. And it was confirmed when I went to his apartment for the first time. We'd been attending our writers' workshop sessions for several months by then, had exchanged lots of books, and he wanted me to see his collection. Mostly women authors. Anne Tyler, Alice Adams, Eve Babitz, Alice Walker, Gail Godwin, Mary Gordon, Alice Munro, Gloria Naylor, Ann Beattie, Margaret Atwood. I'd never read any of these writers until Gary started lending me their books. After I sighed and swooned before the bookcases, Gary produced a photo album. All snapshots of himself. Each one at a beach or by a pool. In skimpy swimwear. His muscles curved and bulged, his skin tanned to a burnished copper. Was he trying to seduce me, turn me on by showing me those pictures? I thought about it for a nanosecond. I'd gladly have my way with his simmering maleness. I suspect my eyes assumed that dreamy look of desire, and I was poised on the edge of vulnerability. I expected him to close the album, take me by the hand to his bedroom and remove my clothing with his teeth. Instead, he closed the album, asked if I'd like some coffee, yawned and stretched. I declined and departed. Never again did I consider the possibility that something sexual might occur between us. And I still can't figure out why he showed me those pictures.

There's no denying that undercurrents of sexuality painted subtle hues in the shadows of our lives. Lenny placed me on the opposite side of attraction in the crucible of seduction. He was slim and boyish, his hair a darker blond than Gary's, but I never once felt a physical yearning for Lenny's body. When we went to the beach and he stripped to his swimsuit, I looked at him with indifference and let my gaze wander to the more muscled bodies on the blankets nearby. When I undressed to my Speedos there was nothing in Lenny's eyes to suggest desire. But one night, as we got drunk in a bar, his lips brushed mine after a confidence was whispered in my ear. I drew back. Was this a sign of passion or merely alcoholic clumsiness? Lenny looked at me quizzically. "No?" he asked meekly, prepared to be let down.

"I don't think so," I said, and immediately regretted my words. Surely there was a more tactful way to decline. I feared my response would sour our friendship.

"You can't always get what you want," he said, and smiled. Then we laughed and hugged and the possibility of sexual contact never entered our sphere again.

We had plenty to keep us occupied. Lenny was my constant companion for theater, music, and film. He was a reader too, but we didn't talk about literature in the same way as Gary and I. Lenny preferred simple books – thrillers, mysteries, and the occasional celebrity tell-all. From time to time he would read something more substantial, and then eagerly tell me about it. He was impressed by literariness.

But monitored his intake like a dieter approaching slices of chocolate cake. After reading Edith Wharton, he relaxed into Robert Ludlum. Occasionally he would persuade me to read something that Gary and the rest of my writers' group considered blasphemous. Like Stephen King or Danielle Steel. My enjoyment of this stuff was minimal but I appreciated the experience because it offered a different perspective compared to other types of books. But when I'd try to convince Gary that he should check out some of the books that Lenny suggested, he remained staunchly uninterested. I was the one in the middle, benefiting from both Gary's writerly sensibility and Lenny's readerly tastes.

I can't recall a single instance when they met. They were like twin moons in different orbits, circling around the planet that is my world. They knew about each other, but only what I would tell. I never intended to keep them apart. But scheduling and the divergence of interests prevented a face-to-face encounter. When I was a child all of my friends knew one another. Every activity involved five or six individuals. But for a long time now, my friendships have been isolated. If I were to throw a party for everyone I know, they'd all have to be introduced upon arrival and would spend the evening attempting to find intersecting points of interest.

If there's life beyond death, maybe Gary and Lenny are buddies now. Could they be lovers?

What would they tell me about sickness and death? Would they advise me to take the test or avoid the witch doctors?

Gary was a computer programmer. Lenny held a degree in pharmacology. When Gary became ill, he sequestered himself and communicated only with his lover. I didn't see him or speak to him at all for the last three weeks of his life. Lenny allowed me to visit him in the hospital twice before he couldn't take it any more and detached himself from the tubes and machines. I wish I could seek their counsel now that the scythe of death sways on spider web strings just above my throat.

* * *

The mailroom clerk, Pedro, makes his rounds, dropping off letters, manuscripts, press releases, postcards, bills, magazines, newspapers, and books. I've been here for almost four hours already and I wonder if today is the day that I'll finally spin out of control and do something reckless. My nervous breakdown could manifest itself at any moment. Thank God it's Friday.

Five days a week, twice each day, I receive a stack of correspondence, some of which is fun to open. Much, though, is either boring or depressing. The latest news about penis enlargement. Astrology calendars geared for gay guys. A baggie with soiled underwear to be forwarded to a porn star. The St. Louis Lesbian and Gay Marching Band will be performing at the gazebo of Our Lady of the Perpetual Heart. A newsletter from the North American Man/Boy Love Association. A brochure from a guest house in Key West. Would I be interested in attending a gallery opening by a photographer who specializes in portraits of geriatric amputees? Could I publish, please, naked photos of Rock Hudson? A reader in New Mexico asks if he should have his foreskin pierced. A writer in Chicago wants to know if I'd be interested in an article on the epic verse of Ethiopia. A scrawled note says: You filthy scum I hope you rot in hell also Jesus loves you you homo pervert. I save this particular gem for my personal archive. There are stories about cowboys, construction workers, truckers, and lifeguards. Photographs of models duded up as sailors, cops, lumberjacks, and football players. A magazine of lesbian erotica. A book about AIDS. Another book about AIDS. I think about mouth fungus, doctors, hospitals, tubes, pills, funeral orations, Gary, Lenny, Donald.

The telephone rings. I welcome the distraction. The caller asks if I'm the editor of *Manmeat*. I tell him that I am. He wants to know if I'm gay. I tell him that I am. He declares that I'm the very first gay person he's ever spoken to. I can tell that he is pleased. I am too. I wish all my calls could be this easy, so rewarding. I return to the stack of mail, and again the phone rings. This time it's a man who complains that the March issue of *Big Boys* doesn't have a single article about AIDS. I point out the safe sex warning on the inside front cover, and go on to explain that there are publications far better equipped to report health issues, and that our readers come to us for entertainment, not enlightenment. He still thinks that I'm evil and the magazines are dangerous, so I continue and highlight the fact that the magazines are used for the safest sex of all, that we run public service ads about condoms. But he utters a few nasty words and slams down the phone. I feel like I'm going a hundred miles an hour down a dead end street with a high wall of red bricks coming closer, fast. I try the brakes but there is no resistance, no slowing down. I close my eyes, try to breathe deeply, grip the arms of my chair. Shaking, I walk to the water fountain and fill a paper cup. Cool liquid coats my throat. I notice that my heart is pounding my chest like a heavyweight champion. Feeling slightly dizzy, I slowly walk back to my cubicle. My hands are too sweaty to grasp the letter opener. I rub them against my denimed thighs. Light a cigarette. Try to slow my body rhythm.

I open an envelope containing a letter and a resumé. Some young man would like to be an editorial assistant. I turn to my typewriter and inform him that there are no positions available at present.

The intercom buzzes. I am summoned to The Boss's office.

He has the biggest space on our floor, of course. Windows facing west and south. A formidable marble desk and a huge round table. I've never seen him at the desk; he commandeers the troops from the section of the table set apart by two telephones, a computer terminal, a fax machine, and a calculator. The office is decorated in mellow shades of burgundy and gray. There are garish paintings on the walls, and an alabaster statue of a Rubens-type woman on a brass pedestal. The Boss has questionable taste.

He is on the telephone, yelling about some plane tickets.

He concludes his call and makes another. Instructs someone not to go above one hundred and seventy-five thousand.

Seated about the table are the Vice President – Valerie; the head of subscriptions – Jeannette; two art directors – Jonah and Tony; and Sheila – the editrix of *Dairy Queens* and *Bad Girls*.

The Boss hangs up the phone and looks at us. He smiles and says, "Ah, my family."

He's a thin, balding man. The effort of smiling looks like it's too much for him. The smile quickly disappears and is replaced by the more familiar scowl of disapproval. "We have a big problem," he says. Pausing, he lights up a cigarette. Valerie mimics him, lights a cigarette in the same deliberate manner. If he asked her to step into a bear trap and swallow a cyanide capsule she'd do it without hesitation. "Our subscription lists are doing very badly. We've lost over nine hundred subscribers in the past year."

He stares at us with contempt. Valerie notes his expression and tries to copy it. The Boss's gaze fixes on Jeannette, head of the subscription department. "Don't look at me. This is Valerie's fault," she said.

"And why is that?" says The Boss.

"Because she insists on ordering the cheapest mailers, which tend to come undone in transit, and the fact of the matter is that people don't like to receive opened mail in any situation, but particularly with magazines like ours, they get really upset. I get several cancellations a day."

The Boss takes a long drag on his cigarette. Valerie does the same. With her lips pursed to inhale, her eyes come together and she looks like a chipmunk. Exhaling within moments of The Boss, she says, "This is not my fault. My job is to save the company money and the mailers we've been using have done just that!"

Sheila, Tony, Jonah, and I argue that in the long run it would pay to use better mailers. Valerie claims that the reason that subscriptions are being canceled is because we don't do our jobs well enough, that the magazines aren't hot enough.

As this is about to erupt into a full-scale contretemps, The Boss silences us with a fist on the table. Informs us that we must create new subscription ads. In the meantime, he will personally investigate the costs of various mailers. Simply put, Valerie wins again. Sheila, Tony, Jonah, and I have extra work.

The boss ditches his cigarette, Valerie follows suit. "Ah, my family," he says. "We have our quarrels but we talk things over and everything works out fine. Good day."

He picks up the phone and asks for his investment counselor.

We file from his office a bit less enthusiastic about life. I hurry back to my cubicle so I won't miss the deadline that's coming at me like bullet.

FIVE

AMAZING HOW SOMETHING AS SIMPLE, something as common as a blood test can change your life. You think you've finally gotten reality within your grasp and then suddenly you find yourself in another dimension of time and space. Looking around, the same sights appear before your eyes, but they look different. Things seem less solid, slightly shifty, colors fade, shapes alter, almost imperceptibly. What once felt like firm ground becomes shaky and unreliable. Words that had meant very little begin to carry the weight of centuries. And thoughts that were easily contained shoot out into space, wandering in the vast uncharted wilderness between the galaxies.

You're slightly nervous before the doctor pierces your skin with the empty syringe. As the blood begins to fill the cylinder you think of deceased friends, hear the tragic echoes of news reports. Body count statistics and photographs of skin lesions appear before your eyes.

You must wait for the test results. Three days, in my case. Every minute is like an eternity as you careen off the walls of hope and fear. Just when you've managed to convince yourself that a cure is beyond the next door, or that you've miraculously managed to escape infection, you picture yourself scarred, emaciated, lying in a hospital bed waiting for the end to come. You think of the pleasures you'll miss, of the pain you must endure. And then you convince yourself that this can't possibly happen. Not yet. Not to you.

The doctor is solemn when he tells you the awful news. He tries to sound hopeful, but the subtext of his speech is heavy with grief; the threnody of a death's-head incantation.

As you attempt to continue with your life, what's left of it, you see the frightening grin of a skull and crossbones in every newspaper headline. The sounds of formerly innocent words attack your eardrums like exploding munitions factories. You begin to notice bodily sensations – pangs, itches, cold spots, warm patches, numbness – that you can't recall ever having felt before.

You become sad. And then you become angry. You want to shout into politicians' ears, throttle medical researchers, destroy government buildings. As you fill out your tax forms you ask yourself why you should pay a tithe to the bureaucracy that perhaps created, and surely sustains, your disease? Would you be terribly surprised to learn that AIDS was born in an American Military-Industrial test tube?

Sirens like cutlasses slice the air with cold precision. Tires melt screeching as brakes jam. The sound of motorcycles is like the mechanical chopping of electric guillotines. I sit in my apartment craving silence, wanting to listen to the distant voices in my head. I can't screen anything out and listen to the noises like music. The sound of a mobile street cleaner is very much like the rustling of clothing and water in a washing machine. How the whirring stiff bristles could resemble the swoosh of wet cloth is baffling. But the sounds take me back. To when I was a child and would fall asleep on the floor up against the dishwasher, its warmth, vibrations, and white noise encompassing me like a comforter. All sound is mysterious. Especially music. When the notes fade from our ears, where do they go?

The sharp ring of the telephone rises from the din like a triangle in the Liszt piano concerto. I have three choices: I can simply take the call and bravely face whatever hassles it might bring, or I can monitor the caller to avoid any unwanted intrusions, or I can let the machine take the message which I will listen to when I'm feeling less vulnerable. What astonishes me is how quickly the situation is assessed and the decision made. I'll risk being bludgeoned by bad news or a repulsive personality in the hope that this call could involve something which will make me happy for a moment. I wish I had an answering machine to screen the calls for me at the office.

I say hello with caution, sitting on the couch, watching the baby bettas flitting about their watery home. I'm breathless with anticipation, imagining that this could be a solicitor from some charity organization, someone selling magazine subscriptions, a wrong number, a phone-sex nerd, some trick I gave my number to before I met Jon.

"Hey, babe, it's me. What's shakin'?"

I'm relieved that it's Dayna. She sounds very cheerful. Talking with her will do me good, especially if we avoid my problems and deal with hers.

"I met someone," she says.

This is very good news. Since she broke up with Martine, about six months ago, Dayna has gone through three distinct phases. Initially, she swore off women, sex, and relationships altogether. Then she actively sought all three with abandon. Lately she's been somewhat subdued, claiming there's more to life than the romance dance.

"Tell me about her."

"Well, her name is Kate and she's beautiful, sexy, and smart."

When I was growing up, lesbians were unknown to me. I suspected that there were a handful of gay guys out there and prayed that I'd eventually meet some. Finally free of my parents when I got to college, I really began to explore the world, as though for the first time, and discovered the invisible tribe of the female sex. It's difficult to describe the elation I felt when I realized that there was a pattern to the madness of human sexuality. Suddenly I felt less freakish. Part of something big and wonderful and mysterious. It was the feeling of having been granted permission by the women's sector that made me feel more comfortable about my inclinations. After all, if it's all right for a woman to make love to another woman, the same must hold true for men.

"Tell me more."

"She's a lawyer and works for a very big firm – a long string of names I don't have down yet."

"Everyone should have a lesbian lawyer," I quip, a line that often came up when Dayna and Lenny and I were together.

"And a Jewish doctor and a gay dentist," Dayna adds, completing the joke. I know she has just thought of Lenny for a moment just as I have. But neither of us will talk about him yet. The scars from his death have not completely healed. "She's from Iowa and has a really spiffy apartment on the Upper West Side."

"Fancy schmancy. What does she look like?"

"Beautiful tawny hair in thick cascades. An innocent face, a slender body with the cutest buns and long legs." We hear the click that means someone is trying to reach Dayna's phone. "That's my call interrupting, I mean, waiting, hold on a sec." It's her mother, whom she does not want to speak to at the moment. "Where were we?"

"You were telling me about Kate."

"Right. It's been great."

"How long have you been ..."

"Dating or fucking?"

"Both."

"Almost a month."

I'm very happy for Dayna. The call from her mother reminds me of all the trouble she had with her family. I don't really understand how family relationships evolve. Why one member is good or bad toward another. As I grew up it seemed to me that my family was abnormally normal. No divorces or separations, no murders or abuse. Fights and arguments were quickly resolved and forgotten. There are no particular incidents I can recall that irrevocably changed any of us.

Not having witnessed Dayna's upbringing, I can't account for the hostility of her mother and two sisters. Dayna is the most warm and generous person I've ever known. And she'll do anything to gain the love and approval of her family. Despite their petty meannesses.

When Lenny first introduced us she still lived at home. And every time I spoke to her she reluctantly revealed new transgressions. Her mother would agree to drop Dayna off at the supermarket and pick her up at a designated time. The first part would work fine. But when the pick-up time had arrived, and then gone, Dayna would walk home with a week's worth of groceries for four people. Her mother didn't apologize or explain.

When I bought Dayna an aquarium, she set it up in her bedroom. Her sisters cracked the glass, intentionally it seems, with a hammer, and watched as the water ran all over the desk, seeped down the walls, soaked the carpet and leaked into the living room below. The sisters denied it and Dayna bore the blame. She even forgave them for killing her harmless pets.

Dayna is so happy talking about Kate, I wish she wouldn't stop. But eventually she sighs and says, "Well, enough about me. What about you? How are things at the Penis Palace?"

"Let's not get into that," I say.

"Well, then, how are things going with Jon?"

"Let's not get into that either."

"Doesn't sound good. What else is happening?"

"I really don't want to talk about this, but I guess I have to tell someone eventually. Might as well be you. I apologize for dropping a ton of bricks on your head, and I hope you're sitting down. I took the test – I'm positive – I have some minor symptoms – I'm on AZT. That's all I can tell you at this point."

I hear her breathe deeply. She has already been through this with Lenny and several others. I hate having to lay this on her shoulders. She asks if there's anything she can do, and of course, there really isn't, but I assure her that I'll let her know if I need something or want to talk.

We say good-bye and I hang up the phone.

The clock on the VCR tells me Jon will be home from the gym very soon.

I was lost and alone. Adrift in a storm of confusion. Unanchored, powerless and afraid, I was spinning and tumbling and didn't know how to stop. Then I met Jon. And realized I'd been in the grip of a kind of seizure.

I suffered from the lack of a strong attachment. Although I'd had lovers and tasted the pleasures of countless men, there was no purpose, no design, no love. I leaped from bed to bed, avoiding the snaggly-toothed maw that threatened from below. The jaws were strong, the appetite voracious. But like an aerialist who never falters, doesn't need a net, I sailed through the air with poise.

Then my friends started dying. The bed-hopping ceased. And I was thrust into more confusion, more longing. Sex became the most desired and least obtainable aspect of my existence. Misery wrapped itself around me like a shroud.

Then Jon entered my world and everything began to make sense, chaos flattened into order.

We met at a party. Just a casual gathering of people, some of whom I'd met when I worked at an off-Broadway box office. I noticed him right away. There was a serenity about him, a quiet brooding quality that immediately attracted my attention. His handsome face was that of a boy-man. His eyes were alert, brown, and warm, his thick dark hair not too styled or too unkempt. He moved with agility, his body evidently well-toned. The animation of his face – the small nose, thick lips, and prominent cheekbones – invited me in, making me feel at home.

We started talking. And I could immediately discern a keen intelligence and sharp wit. We seemed to snap together like the pieces of a puzzle. Sitting on the couch, basking in each others eyes, we discussed some movies we'd both seen, talked about current events a little, then discovered that we both liked to read, and got lost in a long dialog about recent books. We'd unintentionally isolated ourselves from everyone else at the party, and were both surprised to find that we were the last to leave. I wanted to invite him back to my apartment, but that seemed too obvious. So I asked if he wanted to go for a drink somewhere.

We stood in a crowded bar, Jon with a vodka, tequila in my glass. There was some odd dance music playing. It sounded like a band of electronic marionettes toying with synthesizers and percussion machines. Wall-to-wall men drinking and talking, laughing and nodding. I stood close enough to Jon to feel his body heat. We looked at one another longingly. Not too much later we were sitting in my apartment, clinging together in a tight embrace.

That first night we hugged and kissed for a while. Then he left and I tried to sleep. But I writhed and thrashed around, unable to find a comfortable position, unable to stop thinking about Jon. I could still taste his lips, smell his masculine scent. I wondered if I'd ever see him again.

I'm in my cubicle and the telephone rings. The caller identifies himself as Steve Harris. I recall the name. The resume I received and opened just before the meeting in The Boss's office. The guy is looking for a job. I inform him that unfortunately there are no positions available at the present time.

"Oh," he moans, crestfallen. "Can I at least come in for an interview? I'm sure once you meet me you'll see that I can be a real asset to the firm. I'm willing to work hard and I don't want a lot of money."

"Well," I chuckle, "you wouldn't make a lot of money here in any case. But as I said, all positions are currently filled."

"But couldn't I come anyway? For an interview? I'd like to meet you and see the place."

"There's nothing to see except a bunch of typewriters, computers, desks, and file cabinets. Besides, I don't have the time."

"Please?" he whines.

"Sorry. I'll keep your resume on file and if I need to speak to you I'll get in touch."

Valerie walks into my cubicle and hands me a memo. "I've got to run," I tell the caller, "deadlines and all. Bye." I hang up and turn to Valerie.

"New subscription campaign," she says. "Copy on my desk this afternoon," she snaps.

"I don't know if I can finish it by then. I'm totally swamped."

"When I say this afternoon, I mean just that." She scowls and departs. I silently curse her. I wish I had a little figurine to stick pins into. Then I sigh and look at the stack of unread manuscripts, the pile of photo sets, the mountain of copy to proofread. I glance at the deadline schedule on the wall. And shudder in disbelief. I'd love to work elsewhere. But now, with the taint of pornography on my record, no reputable firm would employ me. Moreover, now that I'm HIV positive, if I change jobs my medical benefits will be eliminated. No insurance company will take on a "prior condition." I'm a prisoner and I must obey, unless I want to live in rags on the street, styrofoam cup in my hand.

Perhaps I should just slit my throat. The letter opener is within reach. I could jump out the window. The pavement would solve all my problems. But that is not necessary. The virus in my bloodstream will take care of everything.

Tony walks into my cubicle, says, "What's new?"

I read the memo from Valerie and wave it like a handkerchief of surrender.

"Fuck 'em," he says, "I ain't gonna do it."

"You've got to. We've got to."

In the past we've designed many ads together. I write the words, he arranges them among suitable images and colors.

"They can pay me fuckin' overtime," he says.

"You know they won't."

He shrugs again and extends his middle finger. "Fuckin' cunt!"

I don't like Valerie any more than he does, but language like that makes me uncomfortable. And Tony knows it. So he uses racial and sexual slurs whenever I'm within earshot. The nigger did this. The cunt did that. I've learned to ignore it. He's the kind of guy who'll spend time with someone just because he knows his presence annoys them. I'm waiting for the day when he calls me a kike or a cocksucker.

SIX

"HI, MOM, IT'S ME."

"How are you?"

"Fine," I say, "And you?"

"Oh, you know," she says, "a little of this, a little of that. I went to the doctor yesterday and we talked about the hip surgery. He said we should wait a few months."

"Hip surgery? You never said anything about your hip." I'm almost forty and she's still overprotective.

"I'm not getting any younger, you know."

Once again she makes me speechless. Just as I'm wondering if this is a good time to tell her I'm HIV positive, she says, "So, how are you?"

"I just told you, I'm fine."

"Yes, you said that. But how are you *really*?"

She's fishing, I think. Sometimes it's like she has ESP.

"Really, Mom. I'm okay."

"I was watching Donahue the other day and there was a gay man on – very nice, goodlooking – who said that it would be very unusual for a gay man living in New York City to have escaped being exposed to AIDS."

"You watch too much television."

"When was the last time you went to a doctor? You should take the test."

"I don't want to take the test," I say, as if I hadn't already gotten the bad news.

"There are treatments now. They have this new drug

called ZAT ..."

"You mean AZT."

"AZT, thank you, and if you have the virus it will help."

"If I find out I have the virus I'll be too depressed to function."

"It's better to know for sure, it's the not-knowing that will drive you crazy."

"And what if I do have it," I say, the words almost choking me, "won't it drive you crazy too? You worry too much."

"That's what mothers do. We worry."

It's time for me to change the subject.

"How's Greg?"

"You know, you could dial the phone and find that out for yourself. He's fine. And so is Alison. And the kids. They're wondering when they're going to hear from their famous uncle the writer who lives in New York City."

"I've been so busy lately I haven't had a chance to call. But I will. I promise. And I'm not famous."

"To them, you're famous. And to me."

Time for another subject change.

"Did you play this week?"

"Play? Play what?"

"What do you mean, play what? Golf. You know, the little white ball, the tended greens, those holes in the ground, the numbered flags?"

"Don't be sarcastic. I've been meaning to tell you this. I guess now is as good a time as any."

"Tell me what?"

"I don't play golf any more."

This is pretty astonishing news.

"Why not?"

I imagine all kinds of serious illnesses attacking her body.

"I hate golf. Always have."

I couldn't be more shocked and stunned if she'd told me I'm not really her son.

"I really can't believe this, but you don't sound like you're joking."

"I'm not. I hate golf."

"If you hate it why have you been playing every week for the past thirty years?"

"Because of your father."

"I don't get it. Did he put a gun to your head and force you to play?"

"No. It gave us something to do together and talk about."

"You mean, you pretended to like it, and spent all that time doing it, just to please him?"

"That's right. And now, over a year after he's gone, I can stop pretending."

"I can't believe this. You sure fooled me. I thought you *lived* for golf."

"Not any more."

"What about your friends – Frieda, Shirley, Joan – do they hate it, too?"

"Not as much as I do. How is Jon?" she asks, changing the subject.

I don't want to talk about this, but she's going to find out eventually.

"He's fine. But things could be better."

"What's wrong? Is he cheating on you?"

"No. But it's worse than that. The fact is, I don't really care whether he cheats or not. I think we're finding out we're not as compatible as we thought."

"It happens in every relationship," she reassures me, "people go through phases and stages."

"I don't think this is temporary. I think we really don't like each other. Frankly, since you brought up the subject of cheating, I'm thinking of looking for a boyfriend because I'm not getting any love or affection from Jon."

"You can't do that!"

"Why not? Lots of people have affairs. Straight and queer."

"I hate it when you use that word."

"I know."

"It's different for you," she says.

"Why is it different for me?"

"Because if you fool around you might catch AIDS."

"In the first place, Mom, you've heard of safe sex, right?"

"Oprah had a show on it about three weeks ago."

"And in the second place, you think I should stay with him forever, even though we hate each other, because of AIDS?"

"That's right."

"But we could have gotten it before we even met each other, speaking hypothetically, of course."

"Still," she insists, "it's less risky to stay in a monogamous relationship."

"I have to tell you this – I'm seriously thinking of asking him to move out."

"Give it time, things will change."

"I'll keep you posted."

"Don't do anything foolish. And you'll call the doctor and make an appointment?"

"Yes."

"And we'll talk next week?"

"Yes."

"Okay. Take care. Give my best to Jon."

"I will. Bye now."

"Bye."

Such strange dreams lately. The product of a mind reacting to stress? The effects of a sickness like HIV or a drug like AZT? I no longer have a bloodstream. It's a drugstream. I take pills for my virus, pills for my lungs, pills for my sinuses. And I dream the dreams that make no sense to my awakened mind.

The intercom buzzes me back to the cold atmosphere of my office, my desk strewn with memos and red felt-tipped markers, the photographs on the walls of naked men posing and flexing. Rita informs me I have a visitor. I glance at my calendar and see no appointments listed. She says his name is Steve Harris. The name doesn't register immediately. I walk to the reception area and find a young man with a trim haircut and boyish face. He's wearing a polo shirt and acid-washed jeans. There is an eager look in his eyes.

"Can I help you?" I ask.

He introduces himself and claims to be the person who sent a resume and phoned earlier. Now I recall the name.

"You're looking for a job?"

"That's right."

"I told you we don't need anyone right now."

He's not looking at me, but beyond, over my shoulder, as though he might catch a glimpse of a naked porn star.

"I thought if we met you'd see how intelligent and reliable I am and you'd remember me when you do need someone."

He makes me nervous, not looking at my eyes. I'm inclined to glance over my shoulder to see if anyone is creeping up behind me with a machete.

"I'll keep you on file," I reiterate, "and call you for an interview if I should need you."

Suddenly he fakes a move to the left, then runs past me down the corridor. Rita looks up from her tabloid.

"Should I phone the police?"

"Not yet," I say, and take off after the weirdo running down the hall who pauses to look in the offices with open doors.

As he passes, heads pop out and turn to watch the intruder who has transformed our ordinary, dull corridor into the multi-colored, flashily lit alley of a pinball machine.

"What the fuck's going on?" I'm asked as I hurry past a bewildered accountant. I ignore the question and continue the pursuit.

Turning the corner into the L of a hallway where the subscription and art departments are located, I find Steve Harris standing, staring at an autographed, life-size, nude, full-color poster of a deceased porn star famous for his ability to perform auto-fellatio. Mr. Harris looks like he's about to start drooling. He grins at me, and with child-like innocence says, "Gee, it must be great working here, getting to meet people like Ben Dover."

"I never met him," I say, as a crowd of art assistants and subscription clerks gather.

"You never met him? Why?"

"Well, for one thing he died before I even started working here."

"Died? But his pictures were in your magazine a month ago and there's a new video …"

"The photos and video were shot a long time ago. They're being recycled."

"What about Dick Rammer? You must have met him!"

"Never met him either."

Mr. Harris's face seems to collapse, as though someone had dropped a telephone book on his head. "Is he dead too?"

"No, I've just never met him."

"But I thought …"

"You thought that working here was like being invited to a fabulous orgy every day."

"Something like that."

"Look," I say, with sympathy, "you could have more fun working at Burger King."

The crowd at the end of the hall begins to disperse. I take Mr. Harris into my cubicle and show him my typewriter, computer terminal, file cabinet, telephone, and Rolodex.

"It ain't a party, it's a job. They don't call it work for nothing."

"I see. And all those editorials about sexy guys who want to put their dicks in your mouth so you almost missed your deadline – "

"Fiction. All made up. So are the letters to the editor and the true confessions columns."

"You mean that story from the guy in Wichita who claimed to have been fucked by the entire first string of the Kansas City Royals was just made up?"

"I wrote it myself. Glad to know it was so convincing."

"Well, I'll be!"

We chat for a few more moments, then my intercom buzzes. I pick up the phone and Rita informs me that the police are here.

I walk Mr. Harris to the reception area. There are two officers standing by the desk. A skinny guy who gazes out the window, and a taller, heavier guy who flirts with Rita.

I press the elevator button. The door opens immediately and I push Mr. Harris past the sliding door and wait until it closes before turning to the police officers.

"What can I do for you gentlemen?"

"Report of a disturbance," says the heavier officer.

"Vagrant wandering the building," said the skinny one.

"He ran out of here a while ago," I lied. "You missed him. But there was no damage, no charges will be pressed."

The heavy officer sighs and the skinny officer looks angry. "False alarms prevent us from dealing with real problems."

"I don't know who put in the call, but I apologize for the inconvenience."

The skinny officer notices a poster of a naked woman on the wall near the reception area. He asks if they can look around, and I'm happy to oblige. I give them the grand tour, during which the heavier officer openly enjoys the sight of big breasted women adorning the art department walls, while the other looks shocked and embarrassed. Before escorting them back to the elevator, I offer them some free samples. The heavy officer eagerly accepts but the other guy declines as though I'd offered him a glass of poison.

I don't know which is worse: When Jon is waiting at home for me or when I'm at home waiting for him. Either way there is always a battle of sorts. No real bloodshed. But always tense and unpleasant until I submit to the role of peacemaker. There is so much adversity and negativity at the office, in the news, on the street, within my body, I will do anything to attain some serenity at home. It never lasts, of course. Like cotton candy, it evaporates as soon as you taste it. Still, an occasionally pleasing sensation of sweetness is better than constant, uninterrupted bitterness. This is what I used to tell myself when I was single and cruised the bars every night. Now that I'm chained to a full-time companion I long for solitude and freedom.

Arriving home after another excruciating day at the office, I want to relax for a few moments, then work on my novel. Jon is sitting on the couch. He's wearing briefs and a T-shirt, his arms and legs gymed and saloned into the texture and color of bronze. His face is unlined and innocent. He looks good enough to eat. The television set plays a re-run of a cops-and-lawyers show, the volume is quite loud.

"Hi," I say, unloading my backpack.

"How was your day?" he asks mechanically.

"The usual stuff and nonsense," I say. "And you?"

He can't hear me because the television is too loud. I raise my voice, trying to disguise my annoyance. I repeat myself.

Jon goes into his well-practiced huff-state. He does not want to lower the sound of the television but feels that I have forced him to. So he dramatically, with much extraneous effort, contorts his face as though something is causing him unbearable pain, raises his upper torso to reach forward, lifts the remote control unit from the table, and shakes his head, clucking his tongue as he presses the volume button. When the sound level hits normal he again displays a great deal of effort and discomfort at having to put the remote control down, rearrange himself on the couch, and light a cigarette.

"How are you?" I repeat.

Now that I've ruined his day completely, he ignores me, won't say a word. So I play the game and ignore him.

After exercising and showering I go into the bedroom and sit at my typewriter for a while. Though I'm working on a murder mystery that I've concocted from sheer imagination, I'd like to write an angry diatribe about the mean man in the next room whom I once loved and now hate. But I tell myself that no one would want to read about this, and continue with my detective story. It seems as though Lenny is perched on my right shoulder urging me to continue in this direction, while Gary, on the left one, whispers that I should tell the world about my relationship with Jon. Write it all down, he says.

I glance up at the clock on the old battered bureau left behind by the apartment's previous tenant. It's almost seven o'clock. Jon will be leaving for the theater soon. I have two choices. I can remain where I am and let him leave, still snitty and angry with me. Or I can go into the next room, sit beside him and say whatever is necessary to establish some kind of harmony. I don't want the tension to persist, so I opt for the latter.

He's watching a re-run of a sitcom in which the perfectly handsome father and the perfectly beautiful mother endlessly deflect nasty wisecracks from their perfectly adorable and perfectly spoiled children.

I clear my throat and begin to speak. "Is there anything you'd like me to tape for you tonight while you're at work?"

He looks at me with puppyish eyes that I used to melt under, and reaches for the *TV Guide*. He smiles, ready to forgive me now that I've offered to do him a favor.

"I wouldn't mind watching *LA Law* when I get home tonight."

"Anything else?"

"*Cheers* and *Seinfeld*, if it's not too much trouble."

"No trouble. All I have to do is load the VCR and push a few buttons."

"It won't interrupt your writing?"

"No. I have to take a few breaks anyway. And I might watch *LA Law* myself. Then we can talk about it later."

"Good," he smiles, then returns his attention to the screen.

Several commercials later he gets ready to leave and kisses me good-bye. A perfunctory kiss on the cheek that suggests reconciliation, not passion. I return to my writing, which goes more easily now that I don't feel so tense.

I probe my brain and tap my typewriter and it's like therapy or drugs. While wandering in the world of fiction I don't think about my job, my illness, my fractured relationship. I'm lost in a realm of romance, intrigue, suspense and manageable people.

The telephone rings, and instead of picking up the receiver, I monitor the call on the answering machine. It's a message for Jon which I copy onto a pad. As I'm about to resume typing, the telephone rings again. I monitor and pick up when I recognize Dayna's voice.

After exchanging the usual greetings, interspersed with a few sarcastic quips, she says that things are going well at work, and surprise, she actually had a pleasant telephone conversation with her mother.

"Dahling," she chimes, "you wouldn't believe it. She didn't give me shit about anything. She was so nice and non-confrontational. It was supportive and sweet, like mother-daughter stuff should be all the time."

"To what do you attribute her new attitude?"

"No idea. I mean it's not like she won the lottery or anything, or that I told her I'm going straight and getting married. Maybe she just didn't feel like fighting."

"Good. Who knows? Maybe she's finally come to accept you as you are and this will continue."

"Don't count on it. I'd be happy if we could just be pleasant to each other occasionally. Expecting it all the time would be foolish, based on what's gone down before. But enough about me. What's with you?"

"Same ol' same ol'. I'm like a hamster in a wheel, always running, getting nowhere."

"Have you told your mother yet."

"Hell, no! She's still freaking out over my father. In fact, she told me that she hates playing golf. After acting like a golf junkie for over thirty years. I don't think she's gotten over his death yet. Maybe she never will. I can't drop the AIDS bomb on her right now."

"What about Jon? Have you told him?"

"No. He'll hate me even more than he does now. And I couldn't take any more stress than I already have to deal with."

"You've got to tell him."

"I know. I'm just waiting for the right moment."

"The right moment may never come."

I know she's right, but don't want to admit it.

"How are you feeling?" she asks.

"I'm still adjusting to the AZT. I don't feel as dizzy and tired as I did when I first started taking it. But still, sometimes, I feel like I'm just dragging myself around. It's not even the physical manifestations that are so bad, at this point. It's the constant pressure of knowing I'm sick and dying. I do everything I can not to think about it. But every time I take a pill, or open a newspaper, or turn on the radio, or talk to someone, it's like a giant neon billboard lights up that says: you are TERMINALLY ILL."

"Would you rather not talk about it now?"

"I guess it's good to talk about it sometimes, like with you – you never get hysterical or doomy-gloomy – but it just seems like I can never escape."

Dayna adroitly alters the conversation by telling me about some books she's been reading by Pat Parker, Gloria Naylor, and Judy Grahn. Afterwards, I inquire about Kate and Dayna sighs contentedly.

"She's fine. We're fine."

"How often do you get together?"

"Two or three times a week. It's perfect."

Our conversation is over, I take a pill, turn on the VCR and make a tape for Jon. Then write for a while until *LA Law* comes on.

When it's over I read for a while. Then, in the half hour or so I spend waiting for Jon to come home, I feel myself inching along the sharp edge of a razor blade. The hard metal beneath my fragile skin will cut me to shreds unless I can repel the force of gravity. Jon makes me nervous now. There was a time when the anticipation of seeing him was joyful. But now I can't predict his moods. He angers quickly, often over trivial matters, cools down slowly, and tends to direct his frustrations at me. The continual worrying wears me down. I feel like the inanimate figure in a shooting gallery, at the mercy of anyone who chooses to pick up a rifle and aim.

When Jon arrives, my senses focus tightly, attempting to ascertain his mind-set. Have things gone badly at the theater? Did he get pissed off on the subway? If so, I must be careful. But tonight he seems neutral and I proceed to relay the telephone message that came for him earlier. It's from someone he used to work with, an actor who still works off-Broadway, not as fortunate as Jon, who has advanced to The Big Time.

"Thomas called and asked if you'd like to get together this Sunday for brunch."

Jon looks at me like I've gone insane. "What? Are you joking? I don't have time for off-Broadway losers!"

"He used to be a good friend."

"The operative phrase is 'used to be.' I have progressed. He's been left behind."

"There was a time when you would have jumped all over anyone who said what you just did. You've become a snob. You have no time for anyone who can't further your career. What happened to you? You're not the same person I met four years ago."

"A lot's changed," he snaps. "And you're right. I'm not the same person. Now I'm successful. I've worked too hard to be dragged down by nobodies. I have what I want and nobody's going to take it away from me."

He begins to undress and I have to turn away. I don't like what he's become. It makes me feel uneasy to know that nice people can evolve into monsters. Perhaps my distaste for Jon is connected to something I fear in myself. Would I become as obnoxious as he is if I ever graduated from the small presses into mainstream publishing? I hope not.

I inform Jon that I've taped his TV programs. He thanks me and I bid him goodnight.

It takes some time for me to find a comfortable position in bed. I try to fall asleep, but the events of the day parade through my mind unbidden, reluctant to depart. I'm still not asleep when Jon comes to bed about an hour and a half later. Pretending to be in deep slumber, I'm curious to see if he will cuddle and embrace me. For the first two years of our relationship, whenever one of us went to bed earlier than the other, the latecomer would wrap himself around the sleeper. Lately, it seems like there's a line of demarcation down the center of the bed, across which no man may pass. Sometimes it makes me feel like I'm in a cocoon, that no one can touch me, and that the threads that bind me are too strong to break. Or that I'm in a submarine. Under water. All by myself. If I try to escape, I'll drown.

When Jon gets beneath the blanket, turns his back, and curls into a fetus, I do the same. Back to back, I stare at the shadows on the wall. And the demons in my brain begin their taunting and teasing. How can I tell him I don't want to live with him any more, they howl. And why hasn't he said this to me?

SEVEN

I'M FINALLY ABLE TO CLEAR SOME OF THE STUFF on my desk. For almost an hour I've had no interruptions and I've managed to accept and reject several manuscripts. But before I can make any more progress, the intercom buzzes and Rita tells me to go to The Boss's office. As I walk the gray hallways, I recall when I first met him. He seemed friendly, alert, and displayed an avuncular protectiveness that I found endearing. But it didn't take me long to see through his disguise. Although he projects a pleasing persona when it suits him, the prospect of parting with a nickel reveals his true self. He is a frightened, not terribly bright, tyrant who often sabotages his own desires.

The Boss thinks that the best way to make lots of money is to spend as little as possible. And in many situations that is a wise choice. But sometimes you get what you pay for. There was the time when our offices required a new air conditioning system. Of course, the most inexpensive one available was purchased, not powerful enough to effectively cool the required area. Because the system could not do what was expected of it, breakdowns began to occur, eventually on a daily basis. That this took place during a hot and muggy August didn't help. The computers stopped in protest. Lower-caste employees with no windows in their cubicles began to pass out. Trying to keep everyone working at maximum levels despite the stagnant air, The Boss made his rounds, the mask of familial jocularity in place, exhorting everyone to carry on.

At one point, he removed his shirt to let us know that he would willingly make any sacrifice to keep the wheels of industry turning, and therefore, so should we. The sight of his naked torso – mottled, bony, and tufted – did more to frighten than reassure. Eventually he realized that he'd made an error and bought a better air conditioner. The tragedy is that he didn't learn from his mistake when the company needed a new copying machine. When you calculate the cost of the originally purchased model, and add in the repair bills, it's simple to see that the smart and thrifty move would be to buy the right product in the first place. But The Boss still believes that cheaper is better, and the company constantly loses money in stupid ventures like the one in which hundreds of subscribers canceled due to the use of cheap envelopes.

I walk into The Boss's office, a palace compared to the shanties in which the rest of us work, and sit before his large circular table.

He looks up from his ledgers and grins. "Getting any good dick lately?"

I laugh, which is what he expects of me. I'm supposed to be as obsessed with sex as he is and I'm supposed to think that sex is comical and dirty. I cannot tell him that I'm HIV positive, because he freaked out and fired the last two guys who were honest enough to tell the truth. I cannot tell him that Jon and I haven't had sex in almost two years, because then The Boss will think that my dysfunctional sex life will interfere with doing my job properly.

"Yeah," I say, and try to imitate his leering smirk. "And good ass whenever the fuck I want it."

He laughs, pleased that I'm playing his game. "I'm getting good pussy morning, noon, and night," he sneers. "I love pussy the way you guys love dick."

His constant reminders that he's straight and I'm gay don't bother me nearly as much as his narrow-minded assumption that the only thing gay men ever think about is sucking cock. "I like firm, curvy buns," I say, to remind him that there is more to the world than his worm's-eye view can perceive.

He looks confused for a moment, then nods his head as if a light just went on. The jovial uncle mask slips into place. "I understand we had a visit from the men in blue this morning."

I'm not fooled. I know that something is bothering him and it has nothing to do with the cops.

"That's right. An overly enthusiastic job applicant decided to show himself around."

"I understand you handled it well."

"Someone called the police. I don't know who. There was really no need."

"I get nervous with policemen around."

"If you installed the receptionist behind a wall with a glass window and a buzzer-lock on the door we'd have better security."

"But that would require money," he says.

"Yes, it would."

Scowling like a gargoyle, he lifts a copy of *Manmeat*, turns to one of the stories, then stares at me with threatening eyes.

"There seems to be a theme of incest in this story. I thought you knew the rules!"

"Yes, I know the rules."

I'm referring to the list of taboos we're not allowed to transgress.

"Well," he says, triumphantly. "If you know the rules, why is there incest here?"

"It's not a blood relation. The uncle and nephew are related by marriage. There's no genetic connection and the nephew is over eighteen."

"It's still incest."

"Give me a break," I say, exasperated. "On the one hand you want the magazines to be hot enough so people will buy them – on the other hand you impose all these rules which force us to make them bland and uninteresting."

"Don't you understand!" He's yelling now. "If we go too

far there are certain dealers who won't carry our product. If people can't buy them at their local newsstands then we'll lose money!" His face is as red as a fire engine, a vein throbs in his forehead.

"Do you think the customers are going to complain to the dealers that the magazines are too sexy? You think the dealers sit and read every word and carefully consider what's suitable and what's not? Any smart dealer realizes that if the magazines are more daring, then they'll sell more copies. Most of them are straight anyway and would rather not know what's between the covers."

"Don't you understand? We have serious censorship problems in this country!"

"Only because publishers like you are all too willing to back down if there's a dollar at stake. If you buckle under because of a few fundamentalist preachers threatening boycott, then you're agreeing with them that there's something wrong with a young man who is no longer a minor and an uncle who's related only on paper – we're talking about two consenting adults behind closed doors – what you're saying is that their puritanical pronouncements are acceptable."

Smoke is about to issue from his nostrils. In a moment he will burst in a blaze of spontaneous combustion. "IF WE LOSE ONE SALE BECAUSE OF THIS STORY YOU WILL BE FIRED."

"It's the job of the publisher to fight censorship – not enforce it."

"WRONG! IT'S THE JOB OF THE PUBLISHER TO MAKE MONEY. YOU ARE TO GO BACK TO YOUR OFFICE AND CONTINUE WORKING. NOW!"

Slightly shaken but still together, I walk back to my cubicle taking deep, long breaths. The Boss is a piggy bank. Has no appreciation of aesthetics or freedom. Doesn't realize they are worth fighting for. He doesn't understand about poetry or art. To him, heart and soul are just words in a song. He'd probably chop off his mother's arms if he could find a way to profit from it.

* * *

As I walk the crowded streets I'm doing my best to avoid thinking about the things that might upset me. I look at windows with clothing I can't afford, books that don't fit into my budget, furnishings I'll never own.

A voice calls out my name. I turn and find a former colleague standing beneath the marquee of a movie theater. Brian was my editor at the weekly gay newspaper I used to write music criticism for. We chit-chat for a while, filling in the spaces that have developed in the three or four years since we last spoke. As I'm getting involved in the conversation, Brian's eyes look beyond me. He stops talking and calls out, "ERIC!"

A very good-looking man joins us and Brian introduces me. Several seconds later the line that Brian is waiting in starts to move into the theater. He says good-bye, leaving Eric and me standing there looking at each other awkwardly. As I'm about to offer my hand and tell him it was nice meeting him, he suddenly blurts, "I read your last book and I liked it a lot."

This almost never happens. It's highly unusual for anyone to acknowledge that I've ever written anything. All of my manuscripts seem to have been sealed in bottles, tossed into the sea, and nobody's ever recovered one. For a few seconds I feel like gravity has stopped working. While I'm regaining my equilibrium and thinking of how to respond, Eric asks me if I'd like to go somewhere for a drink. I don't drink alcohol any more and noisy bars are not conducive to conversation, so I make the counter suggestion that we have coffee or tea somewhere.

"I know just the place," he says, and we walk to a small bakery that has a few tables and chairs, red-and-white-checkered tablecloths, Teddy Pendergrass with Harold Melvin and the Blue Notes softly in the background. We order pastries and cappuccino.

"Thank you," I finally tell him.

"For what?"

"Telling me you liked my book. It doesn't happen often. I never know what to say."

"I should be thanking you – it gave me a lot of pleasure."

I'm easily embarrassed, and tend to grin and laugh like a fool when I can't figure out an appropriate response. Fortunately, Eric laughs too, and I'm made slightly nervous by his appearance. He has delicate cheekbones and flawless skin. Big eyes and slightly tousled hair. But it's his lips that captivate my attention. The bottom is thick, the top is thin, when they come together it looks sublime. When he talks I can't seem to look at anything else.

To try to conquer my nerves I start asking him questions. As long as he speaks I can avoid sounding like a babbling idiot. He tells me he lives in Chelsea and comes from Indiana. I ask him what he does for a living.

"I'm a computer salesman. I sell computer systems to companies large and small."

"Do you like it?"

"Yes, actually. I guess it sounds pretty boring. Like a used-car salesman or something. But actually, it's pretty interesting."

"How so?"

"For one thing, I get to travel a lot. But what really makes it interesting is that some companies need a little persuading and others are quite eager. The fun part comes once we start designing the system. I have to learn what the exact requirements are and then figure out which units are necessary and what modifications need to be made. I meet some interesting people and find out all kinds of things about a lot of different types of businesses."

"You're very lucky. My job is probably one of the most tedious, unrewarding tasks on the planet."

"Tell me about it."

I cautiously reveal my role as a pornographer, expecting that he'll get up and run away any second. Most people look down on my profession and would rather not be seen with me – as though I sit around all day jerking off and never wash my hands. But Eric's eyes widen and when I finish he says, "Doesn't sound tedious to me."

"Well," I confess, "it *could* be interesting. We're at a point in time where porn has become very political. But my boss is only interested in money so I don't get a chance to really explore all of the areas that I'd like to."

"How is it political?"

"For one thing, porn is at the very heart of the censorship issues affecting college campuses from coast to coast, and the major broadcast media all over the world. And, also, with AIDS and other sexually transmitted diseases so prevalent, porn provides one of the best outlets for totally safe sex. Some people think porn is useful and necessary. But others think that it makes people do risky things and that I must be some kind of monster."

I don't want to bore this man with my workingman's tale of woe, so I change the direction of our conversation. "Do you read much?"

"Yes."

"Like what?"

He almost seems apologetic when he says, "The last one I read is an older book."

He pauses to gauge my reaction.

"That's okay," I try to sound reassuring. "I read books by dead authors all the time."

We get into a wonderful little discussion about some of our favorites, and discover that we both read a lot of French writers, and coincidentally both love Genet, Sand and Balzac. I feel so completely relaxed and at home talking about this stuff, I'm slightly amazed when he asks, "Would you come over to my apartment – to sign my copy of your last book?"

I couldn't be more agreeable if he were to offer a cure for AIDS.

His apartment, in Chelsea, is larger than mine, neat and not ostentatious. There is a suggestion of Santa Fe style – a Navajo rug, bleached wood table and chairs, a Georgia

O'Keefe print, several cacti on the windowsill. Eric looks firm and nicely proportioned. I guess he is in his early thirties.

He sits beside me on an off-white couch and hands me the book and a pen. I write a brief message and sign it with love.

"I'll read it later," he says, his voice suddenly lowering into a seductive croon. He stares at me intensely and I feel his hand on my thigh. Leaning toward me, his lips touch mine and I feel a jolt of electricity. And then, like a collision in mid-air, my desire went up against my sensibility. I felt like a speeding car crashing into an embankment. Pulling back, away from him, I place my hand on his, hoping he will understand what I must say.

"I can't do this. Please try to understand. I want to but I can't. I'm sick. I have AIDS. I don't want to infect anyone else. I can't believe I'm telling you this. It's something I'm still not comfortable talking about. I have thrush. It's a mouth infection. I want to kiss you but I can't. I don't even know if it's contagious but I can't risk it. I haven't even worked up the nerve to tell my lover yet. That's the other thing. I have a lover. Sort of. We live together but we're not getting along very well lately. I don't know what's wrong with me. You're very attractive. I'd like to. But I can't. I think I'm going crazy."

This torrent has probably astonished Eric as much as it embarrasses me. All I can do is stare at the floor. I release his hand, trying to think of a way to leave without making this situation any more uncomfortable than it already is. I shift and begin to rise.

Eric places his hands on my shoulders and pulls me toward him. He locks his arms around me and buries his face in my neck. I feel tears forcing their way through my eyes. They run down my cheeks as I try to stifle the sobs that begin to shake me. I cry onto Eric's shoulders as he holds me tight, calls me baby, tells me everything is going to be all right.

When I finally conquer the tears and the spasming quakes subside, I pull away, too humbled to even look at him.

"My lover died two years ago," he whispers. "His name

was – is – Darrell. I miss him. And I understand what you're going through. I really do. I'm grateful that you told me the truth. You could have simply said that I'm not your type. But you didn't. I respect you for that. Maybe I can help you. If you ever need to talk about anything, or if you ever need me to do anything for you, just call. I'll be there for you. Really. Can I get you some water. How about some tissues?"

I drink some water and blow my nose. Dry my eyes. Tell him everything I've been holding down deep inside. Thinking back on it later, I wonder why it was so easy telling a stranger what I couldn't say to the people close to me.

Eric tells me about Darrell. The good times they had. How difficult everything became as he grew weaker. The way they helped each other through it all.

He gives me his telephone number and urges me to call him. When I leave I feel as though a demon has been exorcised from my soul. I walk home and can barely feel the concrete beneath my feet.

EIGHT

I REMEMBER MY FIRST DATE WITH JON after the night we met. A movie, *The Fourth Man,* directed by Paul Verhoeven. Interesting that this is where our relationship began. I can follow the trajectory of our rise and fall with the films of Verhoeven as signposts along the way. After Jon and I had been living together for a while, he bought a VCR and we saw *Spotters* while we were still on the upswing, and *Soldier of Orange* when we peaked. Just about the time when things began to go badly between us, Verhoeven released *Robocop.* This was the last time Jon and I did anything together that didn't end with angry words and bad feelings. Since the premier of *Robocop* we've occupied the same apartment, slept in the same bed, but we might as well be living on different planets.

At the time that *The Fourth Man* played in New York, Jon lived in an apartment in Brooklyn. We saw the movie at the Waverly Theater (now a part of some vast corporate chain) just a few blocks away, then walked to my apartment. I showed Jon the things he hadn't seen the first time he came over: the tiny bedroom, the large record collection, the view of Sheridan Square. We talked about the film while I fixed some drinks. Then we sat on the couch opposite the television, Jon lounging like an odalisque right next to where Max and Missy's aquarium would eventually be set up.

The way his jeans hugged him so tightly, his shirt slightly billowy yet revealing his hard chest, the adoring look on his face, the sexy pose, all made me want to pounce. But as

I began to say something about the religious imagery in the movie, Jon encircled me, hugging and kissing, then led me into the bedroom.

We undressed each other and clutched, naked, standing, the warmth of his body like a soothing balm. Our cocks grew stiff between us and we fell onto the bed. Then stretched out head-to-head. I was not certain what he might enjoy. I knew what I wanted. His cock in my mouth and ass, my cock in his mouth and ass. Without any verbal coaching we instructed one another. Through touching, pushing, pulling, stretching, turning, rubbing, patting, we created a new language. And after we'd explored each other thoroughly, I fucked his ass as he jerked his cock. We came together. Then hugged chest to chest. And eventually fell asleep, my front to his back.

I kept waking up all night, unused to having someone in my bed after the sex had ended. It had been several years since Mike moved out. And most of my tricks had departed on their own or by my request. I was not accustomed to sharing my bed. But after several nights with Jon, it once again became natural and familiar. I couldn't recall what it had been like to sleep alone. Beneath the moonlight through my window I watched him as he shifted in his sleep, with his lips gently parted, his hands clasped as though in prayer, curled with knees bent, as vulnerable and endearing as a child.

He stayed with me three or four nights a week. We saw movies, plays, talked about books and music. Had dinners, chatted on the telephone. Walked to the river, through the park.

We were comfortable together. We could understand each other's desires. Not just the sexual kind. Both of us had jobs we detested and longed to establish ourselves in creative areas. Jon is an actor. Prior to meeting me he had performed in dozens of high school and college productions, a few off-off-Broadway showcases, some work as an extra in films, appearances in several commercials. What he wanted most was a big part in a long-running play.

I'd been crawling on the path leading toward literature.

Several music reviews, a few news features, had appeared in print. I'd conducted interviews with several composers and authors. And though I'd written a few short stories, none had as yet been published.

When Jon was finished at the restaurant where he worked, and when I got away from the box office where I earned my living, we'd meet and commiserate. I told him it would not be long before he got the right part. When he went to auditions I wished him good luck and if he failed to land the role, comforted him. He urged me to send my stories to magazines I never would have thought to submit to, and told me to keep trying every time I got a rejection slip.

We talked endlessly. Had glorious conversations that touched on politics, sociology, psychology, philosophy, science. But we always came back to the arts. Jon deepened my appreciation of Verdi, Puccini, Sondheim, the lesser-known films of Hitchcock, Hawks, Sturges. I brought Coltrane, Davis, Ellington, and Coleman to his attention and made him a fan of Altman and Truffaut. We swapped hundreds of books, old and new, respectable and trashy. Jon attempted to instill in me an appreciation for Stephen King, but I didn't get hooked. I had no success trying to get him to fall in love with Jane Austen. But our differences were important. They added texture and richness to our blend. Even when we disagreed, we respected one another, we had fun.

One day we both played hooky from work and roamed the city. We ate a large breakfast in the Village, went to the Museum of Modern Art, had a big lunch on the Upper East Side, gamboled through Central Park, visited the Planetarium, saw a movie, ate dinner in Chelsea, went to see a Broadway play, danced at a private club on Fourteenth Street. Then went back to my apartment and had leisurely, love-filled sex. Drifting to sleep, holding him in my arms, I felt like nothing in the world could ever trouble me.

Now we sleep together, but apart. Never go anywhere as a couple. Argue and rarely talk. I want to feel him beside me in bed. But I fear we will never share intimacy ever again. The physical aspect of whatever it was we had is confined to the past, it would appear. And our friendship is gone as well. In some ways perhaps we have become useful or convenient to one another. How I miss the days when every moment was an adventure, when the beating of our hearts could make a danceable rhythm.

I complete work on a fictional "True Confession" involving two cops and a burglary victim who have rough sex with nightsticks and handcuffs after the latter makes a complaint and the former arrive to investigate the scene. I glance at the clock. It's almost lunch time and I'm very hungry, but I can't go yet because we're allowed out for lunch only between one and two. I hate being treated like a second-grader.

Sheila comes into my office, sits on my desk – well, a small stack of manuscripts and slide holders – stretches and yawns.

"Long day," she says.

"I'm starving."

"Me, too. How much longer?"

"About a half hour."

"I hate this place," she says, scronching her face up like a peach pit.

"Not as much as I do."

"What's new?"

"Same old shit. The cops go to some guy's apartment after he's been robbed and they get into a hot three-way. Ho-hum. What's new with you?"

"Attractive young woman with big boobs goes to the mall to buy a pair of shoes, the salesman turns out to be a foot fetishist and comes in his pants when she presses her toes against his crotch."

"Thrilling."

"What's happening on the home front?" she asks.

"No complaints," I lie. "You?"

"I'm going to break up with Ted." She dramatically sweeps

her hair up and back, then stares at me as though at a camera. "I'm tired of being his mommy. He acts like such a child. Why do I always attract these mamma's boys who are afraid to make decisions, afraid to initiate anything, just plain afraid? They all seem to be afraid of sex unless I make the first move. It's like they think they'll turn me off if they indicate that they really want it. What I wish for is that some brute will come along who'll take control and have his way with me. That would be nice for a change. I'm over the sensitive types."

She pauses for a moment and looks at me to make sure I'm listening. I nod to indicate that she has my complete attention. She always does. One of the few people here I can really communicate with, she always has interesting things to say. "Most people – in this country, anyway – are frightened of sex. And not just because of diseases and stuff. It's just that we're taught from a very early age that sex is evil and the naked body is disgusting." She pulls some lint from her skirt. "We're taught to be ashamed of our bodies and that sex is dangerous. I remember the first time I was told to cover myself up when I was a little girl. I was about three or four. Up until then I was able to run around the house naked and no one seemed to care. Then one day, out of the blue, my mother said that unless I want to be thought of as a slut, I'd better not let anyone see my breasts or genitals – except my eventual husband. I remember seeing her show me how brazen I was by moving her left arm across her chest and placing her right hand over her crotch. I was instructed from that day on that I was not be unclothed in the presence of anyone, anywhere, anytime. Except of course, my husband. If I'd waited all this time for a husband – to just get naked with people – I'd still be a virgin, and miserable. Can you imagine – me, a virgin?"

We laugh.

"That's why there are so many sex crimes," she continues, "so much frigidity, so many closet cases. Before we're taught anything else, we learn to feel weird about sex and nudity." She's speaking more quickly, more insistently. I don't want to break her stride because it's obvious she needs to vent her feelings about all of this. I should know, because I do, too. "And some people never get over that initial propaganda. Most people – like you and me – eventually find out that we've been sold a lot of horseshit and we learn to love our bodies and appreciate sex. But many stay uptight all through their lives. And the thing that scares them most is the idea that children can be sexual. They want the rest of us to believe that a young person never has a sexual urge or a sexual thought until, all of a sudden at the age of eighteen – BOOM!"

"Yeah. It's okay for kids to see movies in which people are tortured and mutilated but love and affection is a taboo."

Tony pops in the door. "Lunch?" He looks at me, then at Sheila.

She and I look at one another. She raises her eyebrows. I purse my lips. Neither of us wants to spend one minute with Tony, let alone an entire lunch hour. But if we decline he'll be nasty and vindictive for months.

"Sure," she says.

"Sure," says I.

He glances at his wristwatch. "'Bout fifteen minutes?"

"Sure."

"Sure."

He leaves and Sheila sticks her tongue out at the space he's just vacated. She looks at me and we giggle quietly. "Scylla and Charybdis," she says.

No one else at our office would know what she is referring to. "Damned if we do and damned if we don't," I say, to let her know that I do.

We talk a bit more about Jon and Ted. Discuss the effort of trying to save a relationship versus just jumping ship. I cannot yet reveal to Sheila a very significant factor in my situation. HIV. I trust her, but if she inadvertently says something that gets back to The Boss, it could be big trouble for me. And the last thing I need is more complications at work or at home.

Valerie buzzes me and sternly reminds me that I have to finish the subscription ad copy by this afternoon.

"Cool your jets," I tell her. "It'll be done on time."

I slam down the phone.

"That was Valerie. Reminding me about the ad stuff we've gotta do. Have you started yet?"

Sheila smirks and shakes her head. "Nope. You?"

"Nope."

We giggle.

Then Tony returns and we leave to go out for lunch.

Are your friends the people who you go out of your way to treat in the best manner possible? Or are they the ones whom you can continually disappoint, knowing they will understand? Some of my friends have been like the former, according me a degree of respect that sometimes amuses. What have I done to deserve the first class treatment? Others were careless, safe in the knowledge that no matter what they did, I'd be there waiting, understanding, supportive, forgiving. I have tried to be the first kind of friend, never inconveniencing my friends any more than I'd want to be put out by them. I used to get very angry with my friend Joey, who was never on time for anything. He'd keep me waiting in movie lines, in the rain, my stomach would torment me while he'd take his time to arrive at a restaurant. When he died I became more tolerant. Once I calculated that Joey's tardiness added up to the time it would take for me to write a novel. Now I'm less angered when people keep me waiting. But when I can, I scurry like a warrior ant, trying to accomplish as much as I can before the scythe of the reaper stops my mad pursuit.

I think these thoughts waiting for Dayna. Not that she's late. I arrived too early.

We sit on wooden stools, Dayna drinking beer from a mug, I sip imported water from a bottle. The place is very unpretentious and everything looks old. There is a clock advertising Coca-Cola that looks like it's been there since the fifties. The tables and bar have wooden surfaces that look distressed – through use, not design. A faded peace sign is pinned up above the jukebox, another relic from another age.

Most of the time we meet in a men's bar or a women's bar, each of us providing the cachet for the other to enter. Tonight we're at a straight bar; we want to be alone. When we're at a women's bar I attract a lot of attention. At men's bars Dayna is the object of curious eyes and inquiries. On neutral ground I suppose people think we're a heterosexual couple and the only stares and double-takes that come our way are from those still unused to racially mixed groups of people. But since there is a greater antipathy to dark-skinned males with light-skinned women than there is to light-skinned men with dark-skinned females, we don't suffer much from unwanted attention.

The music in this place, Furies, is not too loud, mostly Top-Forty hits of the past several months. There is no dancing and no one sings along. Not too crowded or smoky; it's early yet. The crowd will materialize just before midnight. We're ready for our second round and it's her turn to buy. She walks to the bar and I notice several guys evaluating her as she moves. They assume she's straight, not only because she's with me, but because she doesn't look like their cartoon visions of a lesbian. She's slim and curvy, wears tight jeans and a halter top, carries herself like a fashion model. Her dark hair, in a shower of ringlets, frames her face and bounces on her shoulders. When she's at work, as she once told me, she can play the seductive temptress or the tough dyke – whichever role is best suited to the moment. A very successful legal secretary, she knows how to function smoothly in any situation.

I look at the men watching her and dismiss most of them. Only one looks sexy to me and I memorize his features and contours for eventual use in a jerk-off fantasy; perhaps in a magazine, maybe for personal use should I ever start masturbating again.

When Dayna returns I smirk and say, "You're a hit. You can go home with just about any guy here, if you want to."

She laughs. "Just give me two hours with the blond barmaid and you can have all the guys."

"The guys here don't know how to suck dick – or at least, wouldn't admit that they know."

"The guys here don't know how to eat pussy either, at least from the looks of them. Like I said, the blonde behind the bar."

We share a conspiratorial look and Dayna hands me the bottle. We've already talked about her day and mine. And we've agreed not to talk about our mothers. I don't know what's next on the agenda. The only thing I don't want to discuss is disease. Attempting to avoid thinking about phys-ical damage is almost impossible. Death and decay fascinate people, saturate the media. Living in a world obsessed with death makes it difficult to banish depressing thoughts from my consciousness.

"How's Kate?" I ask.

Dayna frowns. "It's over. We broke up a few days ago."

"That was fast. What happened? You don't seem very upset."

"I'm not really. We found out that we don't have as much in common as we thought."

"Is that all you're going to tell me?"

"Well, for one thing, she doesn't identify herself as a lesbian. She's into women and her consciousness is almost there, but not quite. Every time I used the L word she would back away, as if to say, 'I'm not one of *them.*' So I asked her, 'If we're not lesbians, then what are we?' And you know what she said?"

"No. Can't imagine."

"'Friends!'"

"It's sort of funny," I said, "but it's also kind of sad. It's like she can't face the music and dance."

"Yeah, it's sort of funny, but only in retrospect. I didn't laugh. Neither did she. But that wasn't the only thing. She was just a little too New Age for me. You know? I mean, she wasn't into crystals or channeling or any of that stuff, but basically, I guess the best way to describe it is to say that she's into astrology and I'm into astronomy."

"I think I understand."

She runs a finger around the rim of her mug. "Enough about me. How's Jon?"

"He's fine, I guess. Nothing's changed between us. He's either scowling at me or ignoring me."

Dayna tilts her head and gives me a look that says she's shifting into serious territory. "I hate to bring this up but I just can't help wondering. Do you think he's seeing someone on the side?"

She expects me to respond with equal seriousness, but I can't help chuckling.

"What's so funny?"

"I'm sorry. I can't help it. But you've just touched on my new dilemma, which is sort of serious, I guess, but it's also kind of silly, like a sitcom."

"What's up?"

"Well, in the first place, I don't think Jon is seeing anyone because he's so wrapped up in himself and his career that he doesn't have time for anything else. But I sure wish he was fooling around."

"Why?"

"Because I met someone. A wonderful guy. His name is Eric. And we've got the hots for each other. I mean, I've got the hots for him and I think he's interested, too, but so far nothing's happened. Well, something almost happened, but I freaked. He made the move and I backed away. Partially because Jon and I did vow ourselves to monogamy, at least for the duration of the plague. But if I knew he was cheating then I wouldn't feel so guilty contemplating the move."

"Come off it. Everyone cheats."

"Well, not everyone," I say, although I don't know how much I believe this. "But it's not just the guilt. So far I've only seen Eric once. We'd just met and he invited me over and then he pounced. Part of my reluctance was because of Jon, I'll admit it, but part of it was just that I'm not feeling very sexually inclined these days. I mean, I'm horny, but I'm also afraid of spreading the virus, and also of re-infecting myself. I haven't even jerked off since I tested positive, which I'm only mentioning because we're talking about sex. I don't want to get into a discussion about diseases, particularly the sexually transmitted kind."

"I know, I know. Just let me say one thing here. There's safe sex, you know. And there's no reason on earth why you shouldn't be jerking off. I do it all the time."

"I know. You've told me."

"What's wrong," she asks, "Is it that you don't have the urge any more?"

"No. I have the urge. But when I think about sex I think about AIDS. Can't help it."

"That must make things tough at work."

"Unbelievably."

"Get over it, honey. That's what the establishment is counting on. Uptight fundamentalist assholes are hoping that they can drum up enough fear to stop people from having sex. The non-procreative kind."

"You're right. I guess it's politically correct these days to have as much sex as I can. Even if I don't want it. But I do. I want it bad. I'm just scared."

"Safe sex. Have fun and be careful."

"Let's talk about something else."

"I'm ready for another beer and it's your turn to buy."

I go to the bar and fetch fresh drinks. When I return Dayna takes the cold wet mug and says, "I'm so sick of all this politically correct bullshit! It makes me angry. Like drinking this beer. And hanging out at this bar. If Linda and Carol knew that I was drinking alcohol in a straight bar they'd never let me hear the end of it. Politically correct lesbians don't drink. Politically correct lesbians don't spend their money in straight bars. Have you heard the latest?"

"No," I said, "but I'll bet you're going to tell me."

"Sorry if I'm getting too worked up – and I don't mean to take it out on you – but you're not going to believe this." She pauses dramatically. "The newest restriction is that lesbians are not supposed to use anything that is scented. Which includes perfume, underarm stuff, room deodorizers, the theory being that the patriarchy wants to suppress women's natural body aromas. I hear there's a dyke bar in Boston where the bouncer sniffs all the customers and won't allow anyone in who's wearing a scent of any kind. Can you believe it?"

"Well, yes and no. It does seem absurd. But there are also gay men who have nothing better to do than sit around all day trying to decide if it's politically correct to use condoms, or completely abstain from sex, or smoke cigarettes, use drugs, eat meat, out celebrities. It goes on and on. I'm tired of people telling me what to do."

"Same here," she declares, slamming down the mug a bit harder than she intended.

"If I want to smoke, I smoke," I say, lighting a cigarette. "I do believe in boycotting manufacturers who fund anti-gay politicians, and I do believe in outting hypocritical politicians who indulge in gay sex and then support anti-gay legislation."

I think everyone should be outted. Especially media stars. No matter how untalented they are. They are America's heroes and if the straights knew how many of their favorite entertainers were queer it would change their minds about a lot of things."

"But what about people's right to privacy? When I came out to my parents it was on my terms. I primed them and chose the right moment and the consequence is that they took it pretty well and still spoke to me. If they'd heard it through the grapevine, or whatever, it might not have gone so well."

"That's true," she says. "However, you are not a coast-to-coast star on television every week or in blockbuster movies and you don't influence millions of people."

"As much as I hate to admit it, that's true."

We decide not to have any more drinks and we leave the bar as it begins to fill up. Dayna gives me a strong hug and tells me to take care of myself. We kiss and separate.

I walk back to my apartment and notice the hunks prowling Christopher Street, cruising for sex. I feel a warm sensation in my crotch and when I arrive home I strip and fantasize about the good old days and jerk off. First time in months. It feels so good. I decide to do it again. The second time I think about Eric. It's better than the first time. I finish just in time to clean up before Jon comes home from the theater.

NINE

OUR COMPANY OFFICES ARE ON THE PERIPHERY of Soho, site of a thousand art galleries and a million lofts, and we frequently lunch in one of the dozens of semi-fashionable eateries for which the area is known. There are a handful of affordable, decent places, several very expensive ones, and many dives, avoided by those concerned about their health. During weekdays, in the early afternoon, the very expensive places and the ones with moderately priced fare fill up with tourists and women from the suburbs, taking a break from their indefatigable search for art. You can see them with a *Gallery Guide*, checking off the places they've already been to, and taking note of the ones that remain to be scrutinized.

I sit with Sheila and Tony, waiting for the waiter, the voices from the tables around us rising and falling like the red line of an electrocardiogram. The restaurant has wobbly wooden tables and chairs, a long bar, and abstract paintings on the exposed brick walls. A tape of Motown hits plays softly in the background and all of the waiters, waitresses, bartenders, and busboys wear black.

Eventually a waiter brings us menus, asks if we'd like anything to drink. Vodka for Tony, Perrier for Sheila, Pepsi for me.

Tony says, "I hear you had a visitor this morning," referring to the over-eager job applicant, and I nod as he explains what happened to Sheila, who was in a meeting at the time.

"That's nothing," she says, after Tony's mostly accurate

retelling is completed. "Back before you came along," meaning me – both Tony and Sheila having been employed several years before I was hired, "I had a similar experience, but worse!"

The waiter brings our drinks and takes our order – burgers and fries for all.

Sheila continues, as Tony tries to eavesdrop on the tables surrounding us.

"Some guy called up and said he was a photographer and wanted to show me his work. I was just starting out in the business and didn't know the first thing. So I made an appointment with him. I've since learned that you must ask them to send their work in first and then they can make an appointment to see you, thereby avoiding phonies and no-talents. Anyway, this guy shows up and it's obvious right away that he's not a photographer – he didn't even bring an empty portfolio. He just wanted to meet me and talk about sex. Well, I got really pissed off – I mean he wasn't even cute – and told him to get lost. As it turned out, he waited outside the building until I left and he followed me home! On the subway! Not ten seconds after I closed the door, he buzzed, claiming he was from UPS and had a package to deliver. So I buzzed him in and when he got to my door and I looked through the peep I saw it was him. I got so angry. I threatened to call the police. Then I got scared. I mean – what if he had a gun or something! Anyway, we talked – through the door, of course – and it turned out all he wanted was one of my bras."

"One of your bras?"

"Yeah. I guess to sniff it or lick it or try it on – I don't know, all types read my 'zines – but I refused to open the door. So he gave me his address and I mailed him one and then got a thank-you note a few days later and that was the end of it."

The waiter approaches a table of art collectors – situated just so that all three of us can see them. Tony shushes us and cranes his head to listen, urging us to listen as well.

The first lady orders gazpacho and a tuna salad sandwich. The second, wearing a turquoise scarf and an orange brooch, says, "I want the turkey sandwich. Is it turkey breast or that pressed turkey roll stuff?"

"It's turkey breast."

"Do you have sourdough bread?"

"No. White, whole-wheat or pita."

"No sprouted seven-grain?"

"No."

"How about rye?"

"No."

"Okay, make it whole wheat. Now, do you have low-fat mayonnaise?"

"No. Just regular Hellmann's."

"What kinds of mustard?"

"Dijon. Grey Poupon."

"Darn! No Gulden's or French's?"

"No."

She smirks to her companions. "What kind of a low-rent joint is this anyway?"

Then to the waiter, "Okay, give me the turkey breast on whole wheat, with mustard, but make sure there's not too much, just a little, in fact, you better put the mustard on the side so it won't be dripping out, and lettuce and tomato and American cheese, and make sure the lettuce is thoroughly dry and not wet, I mean really dry; okay, now what kind of American cheese do you have because if it's Kraft I don't want it, I want the kind that gets sliced on the premises."

"I'm not certain about the cheese, I'll have to check with the chef."

"Okay. If it's the pre-sliced stuff I don't want it, but if it's the other kind I do."

"Very good." He turns his attention to the next lady, in a purple scarf with a mauve brooch. But the lady in turquoise and orange says, "I'm not finished."

"Yes?"

Sheila whispers, "This guy is a saint. I'd've killed her by now."

"I also want French fries. But not on the same plate as the

sandwich. On the side. And make sure they're not too greasy – pat them with a paper towel if you have to and if you could pick the more well-done ones for me – I hate the ones that are undercooked and too squishy and mealy."

"Will that be all?"

"Can you believe this fuckin' bitch?" says Tony, a bit too loudly.

"Shh! She'll hear you," I say.

"Who gives a flyin' fuck!" He finishes his vodka in one gulp.

Sheila and I trade glances.

"And I'll have a diet Coke."

"No Coke, but we have diet Pepsi."

She looks at her companions as though an icepick has pierced her heart. Then turns to the waiter and says, "How about diet 7-UP?"

"No 7-UP, just diet Sprite."

"I'll just have water."

As the waiter proceeds to take the next order, Tony says, "Can you believe these fuckin' cunts?"

Sheila and I wince and neither of us have a response to this query. I try to focus our attention back to our table by asking Sheila, "Do you often get requests for bras?"

"I regularly get requests for shoes and stockings, but that was the only time for a bra."

"And do you usually honor these requests?"

"Not anymore. But back then I was so naive. And things were so different."

"Things were a lot fuckin' different!" says Tony. As soon as he's said this, he cocks his head toward another table and sneers, "Get this."

Sitting adjacent to the art collectors are a young artist and a gallery owner.

"It's gonna be a hit," says the owner. "Top of the charts as they say in rock 'n' roll land. Picture on the cover of *Time* and *Newsweek*."

The artist looks embarrassed. "You think so? I think my

politics are too radical. Yesterday no one knew I was alive."

"And now you're a star-in-the-making. Soon to be a superstar. It's because of the balance, the symmetry, the harmony in your work. Your themes reflect a certain lyricism at the same time that they capture the gritty insistent rhythms of the downtown scene."

"Gee. I don't see my work in that way at all. And so much is happening so fast."

"Look. Bartlett and Schnabel are has-beens. With Haring and Basquiat dead, and now that Kostabi has alienated everybody, you're gonna be the one!"

I attempt to draw our attention back to our table. "How were things different before I came along?"

"Well," says Tony, "for one thing, we didn't have so many fuckin' restrictions. We used to be able to show insertion shots and come shots and mild S&M was allowed. Now our stuff is so fuckin' vanilla, calling it porn is a crime!"

"Welcome to the world of pornography, post Ronald Reagan and Edwin Meese," says Sheila.

Tony turns to listen in on two ladies who have been seated right next to us. Sheila and I can't help but hear.

"Bert and I were having lunch at the club with Irma and Walter and I was so embarrassed! It was buffet day and they loaded up their plates with enough food for ten people. They didn't finish half of it and Bert and I just looked at each other in utter disbelief. What a waste! And then, if that wasn't bad enough, Irma took four different desserts and only ate one bite of each! I couldn't contain myself any longer so I finally said, 'Irma, four desserts?' She just looked at me with that innocent look of hers and said, 'I can afford it – it's fixed price.' Well, I was enraged. With all that waste it drives up our membership fees!"

Her companion says, "I remember when Irma and Walter invited us over for dinner and she served Chinese take-out – *still in the cartons from the restaurant! She didn't even take the time to put the food into serving bowls!*"

The waiter brings our food. With our mouths full, we

don't speak and can hear everything at the surrounding tables.

When we're finished we pay the check and walk back to the office.

I stop by the water cooler and surreptitiously take an AZT capsule before returning to my cubicle.

I moved to the West Village over ten years ago. When I was young and naive. The world was a different place. Now I'm a different person. Change is inevitable. When I first moved into my tiny apartment on Christopher Street, in the heart of Sheridan Square, I thought I'd found paradise. Everyone was beautiful and healthy. The economy appeared to be in good shape. Lesbians and gay men were attaining political clout, establishing a body of literature and a communications network. One heard of anti-gay violence on very rare occasions. There didn't seem to be much to worry about, aside from what to wear on Saturday night, which contingent to join in the pride march, wondering whether to bulk up or slim down, which gym attracted the hottest guys.

And then, like a tsunami of polluted water, something washed over Christopher Street, destroying its vibrant colors, leaving behind the detritus of tragedy and despair. The first thing I noticed were the new neighbors. Whereas previously my building's occupants had all been gay men, they began to disappear and their apartments were taken over by straight American yuppies and straight European heirs and heiresses. I didn't know at first that my neighbors were early victims of AIDS. There was no such thing. Someone had gotten sick and returned to his home town. Or had become hospitalized for an undisclosed, obscure reason. There was no pattern yet. Small, friendly, gay businesses began to close. The retail locations were taken over by faceless chain stores, parts of large corporations. The people employed in these places were businesslike and humorless. The merchandise was unattractive. Prices rose.

I'd go to my favorite bars and see smaller crowds. Familiar faces were mysteriously absent. Unsettling rumors began to circulate. At first the perpetrator was GRID – Gay Related Immune Deficiency. The straight press announced the appearance of a gay plague. Two of the guys in my writers' group developed symptoms and died. What was causing this?

Everybody wondered, but we had no evidence, not a single clue. Maybe we were partying too much. Overindulgence, too much booze, too many drugs, poor eating habits, not enough sleep. Then the culprit became poppers. Amyl and butyl nitrate. Everyone I knew stopped using them. But the death toll mounted. Hospital beds were booked solid. It was suggested that, perhaps, gay men shouldn't swallow cum anymore. Or, at least, not as much as we'd become accustomed to. Religious fanatics seized the opportunity to declare that God was punishing us for not marrying and having kids. For engaging in unspeakable acts. But before long those unspeakable acts were blazoned in the headlines of the national press, were discussed candidly by the Barbie and Ken dolls of the network news programs. Eventually, somebody, somewhere, figured out that there was a strange new virus. That it was transmissible through bodily fluids. GRID became AIDS. The party on Christopher Street was over. Nobody joked any more. Hospital visiting and memorial service attending supplanted dancing at the disco, cruising at the bar, pumping at the gym. Some people continued to do what they'd always done. Many others went through drastic changes. Discovered health foods, healing crystals; they searched for God, moved out of the city, pretended they were straight. The death lists grew longer. People began sewing panels for a memorial quilt. It became so large you could pave the entire street from Sixth Avenue to the Hudson River and still have enough panels left to cover the walls of all the buildings.

My world is like a different planet now. Lenny, Gary, and Donald are dead. Others as well. Max, the guy I used to buy marijuana from, is still in Nashville as far as I know. And if he ever cut a record there, I haven't heard anything about it. Jennifer and her daughter, Magda, moved to Los Angeles. I get cards from them on Chanukah and Rosh Hashanah. Mike broke up with me and moved away when he got a job offer from the opera company in San Francisco. He called a few times after relocating but I never hear from him anymore. I wonder if he's still alive?

Change is constant. Evolution continues in spite of the believers in superstition. People learned how to live with tragedy. How to cope with fear and despair. Support groups sprang up. Money was raised for research. Lesbians taught gay men how to survive. Straight folks, a select and wonderful few, displayed sympathy. Meanwhile, a new generation of young gay men arrived in the West Village. Young men with vitality, dreams, good looks, and the will to live. The older guys whose lives had become topsy-turvy found stability among the younger men who came of age during the crisis years, who, unaware of any other way of living, learned to cope. Sex is not evil, they could remind us, just be careful.

Some new bars opened. The streets became ours again. When the fag-bashers began to get bold, to slither from their slimy lairs, the young gay guys and fledgling lesbians fought back. There was a new war to win, along with the battles over fear, ignorance, and indifference. The West Village became ours again. It belonged to us, the lesbians and gay men who'd created it, nurtured it, restored it. The baseball bats of the bashers were met with bottles and bricks. Nightly skirmishes became common. Some people got hurt. A few were killed. Every night people marched in the streets. Chanting slogans like "WE'RE HERE, WE'RE QUEER, GET OVER IT!" You could hear the sirens wail and the tires screech. Windows were broken, cars were overturned and torched. The emergency ward was packed with bloodied combatants.

But now the streets belong to us again. We paid for it with our muscles, our brains, our bodily fluids. It has our names written all over it. Our blood fills the cracks in the pavement. It's ours and we're never going to give it up.

* * *

I try to listen to music. The Billie Jo Spears album Lenny and I would sing along with when we were stoned. Before the first song is over he comes to me, sits beside me, puts his arms around my waist, his head on my shoulder.

I miss you so much, I tell him. And I'm living in hell. The same hell you endured before you died. I hope I don't get meningitis and suffer the same way you did. And I don't want to have to go through the pain and misery of Gary's last few months either. I'm scared. Too scared to live.

And I think I'm losing my mind. Nothing makes sense to me any more. I tell my mother that I'm going to start cheating on Jon and that safe sex is the ticket. Then I tell Dayna that I'm not capable of cheating, and that the rubber and plastic of safe sex is not good enough for someone spoiled by the taste of real flesh. At least I've started jerking off again. It releases some of the pressure.

When I'm fantasizing I don't think about death and disease. And during those brief seconds of bliss, when my body spasms and my mind disappears, I'm free of gravity, worry, obligation.

Cheating. It's because of you, Lenny, that it's so difficult. You made me a moral person. With your patience and understanding. You know what I'm talking about. You must remember what happened with Karl. The triangle. You and Karl and me.

Remember? That day at the beach. Just the two of us. A perfect day for sun, sand, and surf. It was in July. About six or seven years ago. After we'd spread the blanket, unpacked, and shed our clothing, we lay beneath the blue warmth. Cooling breezes lifted our hair, dried the perspiration. We swam, greased our bodies, sipped cold beer, and snacked on deli sandwiches.

And then, after I was settled in a mood of comfortable passivity, you hit me with the accusing words that you'd been thinking about for I don't know how long. My insides knotted.

You knew about Karl and me. That he'd come to my apartment and that we'd had sex. You told me that at first you were so angry you could have killed me. But then you realized that Karl was probably fucking everyone in town. And that you and I were too close to let Karl foul up our relationship. I'll never forget that, Lenny. You placed me above your relationship with Karl. I've probably never had a better friend.

I was so angry at Karl. At first. For telling you after he'd promised me he'd keep it a secret. And then I got angrier still for putting myself in a position in which he could use me to hurt you. I felt so bad. I would never intentionally hurt you. I thought I could trust him. Stupid me. How could I believe someone who was in the act of betraying a friend?

But you forgave me. And the bad feelings passed. We talked it out and before we left the beach that day we were closer than we'd ever been.

But situations like this one can never be completely erased. They leave scars. In some cases the scar tissue can make the organism stronger. Wiser. After what I did to you I could never take sex for granted again. I'm on higher moral ground now. I know how sex can be used as a weapon. It's a serious matter. Now I know.

Lenny rubs my back and nuzzles my neck. In my ear he whispers the words to "Misty Blue" as Billie Jo starts to sing it. When the song is over he hugs me. Tells me he still loves me. And disappears as the next song begins.

TEN

I CAN RECALL WHEN THE FIRST THING I'd think about when I opened my eyes in the morning was what had to be done that day. Household chores or meeting deadlines at work. Now my initial thoughts are about health and mortality. Getting out of bed is like jumping from a plane, hoping my parachute will open and that I'll roll gently on impact before somersaulting to stand and walk away unharmed.

Life was as bright as a garden of origami flowers, interesting edges, angles, and colors of shiny Japanese paper. A field of glistening confetti that stretched so far I couldn't see the end. But so much changed so quickly. Dry, faded flowers in a family album and newspaper clippings with torn edges, yellowed with age, are all my eyes can perceive.

There are times when I laugh and momentarily forget about my time and place. Brief seconds that conjure the magic of excitement and expectation. A joke or a song or a picture or a sexy body can transport me. But I always come back, always too quickly, to pondering my fragile condition, my uncertain future.

I look at the sky to try to see tomorrow. And too often it's the negative of the photo, with the light and dark contrasts reversed. I must stop for a moment and transpose the image into a positive print. And it is this act of translation that leaves me feeling enervated and sad.

* * *

When Jon and I had our long, serious talk to decide whether we should live together, money and health were paramount issues. I remember the conversation so well because money and health have since become like twin prisons. With the cost of professional health care skyrocketing, there is no escape. The best you can hope for is to be distracted from the steel bars and concrete walls for a few seconds at a time.

But back then I did not dwell so much on these enclosures. I found joy and distraction everywhere. I thought Jon and I would live together forever, that our love would be everlasting, that we would provide for one another until we mellowed into maturity and softly faded away.

We sat on the couch in what was still just my apartment, after a strenuously satisfying nine innings of sex, sipping brandy, smoking cigarettes. I had thrown on an oversize shirt to avoid a chill. And I looked at Jon, completely naked still, his body shimmering with a glaze of sweat, all of his actorly defenses down, as sweet and innocent, relaxed and contented, as I can ever recall him. We felt so good nothing could have harmed us then. We'd chase the demons away with our laughter, hold the evil spirits at bay with a kiss.

All of our words were tentative; as though we wanted to communicate but were afraid of sounding foolish.

His eyes became wide with sincerity and he said, "I think I love you."

"I love you. For sure."

"Me, too."

We stared at each other, smiling, then grinning, and eventually we laughed. Uncontrollably. For several minutes.

"What," I said.

"What," he said.

We weren't asking questions, just groping for a way to begin to say what was eventually said.

"Have you thought about us?" I asked.

"Yes. Have you thought about us living together?"

I was very grateful that our thoughts were travelling parallel paths. "Yes," I said, "but I've been afraid to mention it, afraid that it might chase you away."

"Same here. But I finally started thinking that life is short and that I should just take the chance. This seemed like the right moment."

This was happening more smoothly than I'd dared to imagine. "Where would we live? I can't really afford anything more expensive than this place."

"If we live together we'd both cut our expenses in half."

"That's true," I said, but in reality, that is never quite the case, a lesson I've learned.

I didn't want to move to Brooklyn and suspected he would like to live in Manhattan. I had to be the one to do the inviting. "We could live together here. At least for now. I know it's small. But when you get your first million from Hollywood and I get my first advance from Random House we can move to a bigger, better place."

He smiled. And melted my heart with the warmth of his gaze. "Sounds good. And for the time being we'll both have more money than we do now."

"We can fix this place up a little," I said.

He tested me to see if I'd object to changes. "How about if we get rid of that ugly curtain, paint the walls, and face the couch toward the window instead of the fireplace?"

"Sounds good to me," I said, not knowing that these things would never be done. "I don't want you to feel that this is my place and you're just visiting. Anything you want to do here is fine. It'll be *ours*. Completely. Totally."

We were both feeling so good about how easily this was coming together, we became secure enough to move on to other serious matters. Since he'd had the courage to mention living together first, I accepted the responsibility of initiating the next topic.

"There's something else we should talk about. And it's a delicate subject, but I'm going to skip the preliminaries and cut right to the, uh, meat of the matter." I paused, more for the breath than dramatic effect. "As you know, there's a plague going on out there," I gestured at the window, "and I think the wisest thing we could possibly do at this point in time is not have sex with anyone else and thereby lower our chances of getting infected."

Of course, we knew that either or both of us may have already been exposed, but that did not need to be said.

"You're right," he said. "And I agree. We're totally compatible in the bedroom department," he tickled me. Flashed his devilish smile. I pinched him and we rolled on the floor, calling each other silly little baby-talk names.

For the next several weeks, every time he came to see me, he brought some of his appliances and furniture. I began to make space for him. I threw out a lot of junk that I'd been accumulating, mainly old magazines that I always meant to read but never got around to. I even found a few things that belonged to Amos, and some of Mike's clothing, I guess it's difficult to remove everything left behind by former lovers.

When I told Gary about my plans with Jon, I brought him some bookends I'd had since childhood and hadn't used in years. I knew he could make use of them on his mantel, to accommodate his growing book collection. Lenny got two cartons of records I'd received when I was a music critic and had never listened to. Donald carried away an old worn and frayed easy chair that he loved to collapse into and I rarely used. And Dayna had always admired a lamp that my parents bought for me when I moved in – a lamp I had no taste for – so she gladly gave it a new home. I donated old clothing to the Salvation Army, sold books to the Strand and records to Vinyl Mania.

Jon and I discussed the possibility of sharing the lease but decided not to, a good decision in retrospect. We'd split the rent down the middle. And we did open up a joint banking account. It was decided that we would divide up the household chores, with Jon doing the dishes and me keeping the refrigerator stocked. Both of us ate most of our meals at work so the washing and shopping did not amount to very much. We would take turns cleaning the bathroom and doing the laundry. All bills – rent, gas and electric, grocery and telephone – were to be split down the middle except for long distance calls.

It all seemed so logical, so easy, so natural, there was no reason for either of us to think it could ever be anything less than perfect.

AZT capsules are like miniature submarines that enter my bloodstream and launch their torpedoes which explode upon contact with HIV organisms. The only problems are that although AZT wins occasional battles, it can never win the war. And while the skirmishes are being fought my body sustains damage with every launched missile. Prolonged use of AZT causes deterioration of bone marrow and muscle tissue. I attempt to live a normal life as I wonder which will kill me first: the disease or the treatment.

I never liked diseases but I used to like drugs a lot. I would still like drugs, actually, if I were still using them, but I'm so afraid of causing any further damage to my immune system, I stopped. When I refer to drugs, I mean the recreational kind. This is a very complicated subject because the government and advertising media, not to mention big business and big religion, have effectively muddied all of the issues and facts. They make no distinction between marijuana and crack. Alcohol and tobacco are socially acceptable while cocaine and poppers are not. People can't believe anything about drugs because the messages are so contradictory. You have to figure it all out for yourself. Like I did when I was in college. Some drugs are good for you and others are bad. Some make you feel like a god, others make you want to die. But the simple truths are rarely spoken. Silence and darkness, ignorance and prejudice always invade any public discussion.

I can't imagine what my life would have been like if I hadn't experimented with the forbidden herbs and chemicals. They could keep me up all night, if I wished. Put me right to sleep if that was my desire. Make me horny, make me not horny, make me see things that I ordinarily would not have seen, make me laugh for hours. I wouldn't trade those years for anything. If it weren't for HIV I'd still be getting high.

But now I use AZT. The killer torpedo. When I began, for the first three days it made me feel a little speedy. Hyper. I couldn't fall asleep. Perhaps this was psychosomatic. I don't know. Then I went through a phase of feeling slightly dizzy, then a period of feeling tired. Eventually I began to feel normal again. Now I have to pee a lot. And I also take a drug called Zovirax. My doctor said it has something to do with preventing blindness. And whenever I have an appointment, the doctor shoots me up with something called Pentamidine. It's supposed to prevent tuberculosis and other respiratory ailments. I'm not certain if it's the AZT or the Zovirax or the Pentamidine that makes me pee a lot.

Life is not so simple any more, not like the days when I could predict exactly what would happen with each drug I took. Speed, downs, hallucinogens, cocaine, were all so reliable. I felt very much in control. Now I feel like a lab animal at the mercy of a mad scientist.

I stare at the typewriter, trying to think of a clever phrase that will induce people to subscribe to my magazines. I'm not a big fan of advertising. If I want something and I can afford it, I buy it. No jingle or commercial or catch-phrase will make me buy anything. And I don't wait to find out what's available. I make it my business to be aware of what's produced and where I can find it. I don't rely on marketing drones to keep myself informed.

It's not easy to create advertisements, particularly if you think they're pointless. This is, perhaps, my least favorite part of the job. Especially since I've done this too many times already. My conscience won't let me repeat myself. It has to be fresh. I stare at my typewriter. Eventually something will manifest itself in my cerebral cortex.

The intercom buzzes. Valerie summons me to her office. Not as ornate as The Boss's, but not as austere as mine. She has a coffee maker and a tank of tropical fish. Nowhere nearly as attractively seascaped and planted as the aquariums at home.

Valerie sits in her big chair. Regally. She fancies herself an omnipotent warrior. A cigarette bounces on her lower lip as she greets me. Another habit she picked up from The Boss. Only she's not as adept as he. When she attempts certain consonants it falls into her lap. As she tries to be nonchalant about brushing the ashes off, she says, "Where's the new subscription ad?"

"I'm working on it."

"It has to be done today!"

"If you would stop bugging me about it maybe I could find the time to get it done."

She scowls. This is not the response she wants. She would like me to say, yes, great and powerful one, it will be done today because you are a goddess and I will do anything to please you. But I don't give her the satisfaction. I never will. Not as long as she continues to treat me like an ungrateful slave.

Due to my recalcitrance, she redirects the attack. I'm familiar with this tactic. She learned it from The Boss.

"Why are you sending out so much stuff for copying?" She clutches a handful of bills and waves them at me. "We're spending too much on outside copying!" she snaps.

She expects her sharp tone to make me quiver and quake, but I remain calm when I say, "The reason why we have to send so much stuff out to be copied is because the copy machine on the premises breaks down just about every other day – as you well know – and all of our material has to be copied before it's sent to the color separator."

"WE'RE SPENDING TOO MUCH ON OUTSIDE COPYING!" she reiterates, louder, perhaps expecting a different response from me.

I suppress the desire to inform her that I'm not hearing

impaired. But take the opportunity to point the accusing finger at her. "The Boss insists that all of our material must be copied before we send it out, right?"

"Right!" she barks.

"And the copying machine breaks down several times a week, yes?"

She says nothing but lines of tension begin to form around her eyes.

"And if I don't send the stuff out to a copying service I'll miss the deadline and The Boss won't be happy. Correct?"

She remains silent, and the lines deepen as her complexion turns scarlet.

"If you had authorized the purchase of an adequate copying machine instead of the cheapo-cheapo model that was not built to accommodate our needs, we wouldn't have all these bills to pay, would we?"

I can see that she's trying to think of another topic upon which to snag me. She is well-practiced in the art of pretending that real problems don't exist and creating phony problems as smoke screens, something else she learned from The Boss, who picked up this strategy from Ronald Reagan and George Bush. The Boss and Valerie will claim that they didn't eat the cake as they wipe the chocolate from their lips.

"Your magazines aren't selling well enough!" she finally says, certain that she's caught me.

"That's very interesting," I say. "Then maybe you should discontinue them and start up another business. Like needlework or bricklaying."

"That's not funny! If the sales don't improve we'll have to cut your budgets."

"If you cut the budgets, the magazines will sell even less than they already are."

"I don't like your attitude!"

"It's genetic. Write a note to my mother. It's all her fault."

"GET OUT OF HERE!"

I return to my cubicle, the typewriter, the subscription ad.

ELEVEN

THERE'S A PECULIAR FEELING THAT ALWAYS OVERTAKES ME on Sunday mornings. It's a remnant of my childhood, I think. Sunday school. Most retail businesses in our neighborhood are closed. Father is not at work, not playing golf. The huge *New York Times* takes up the morning. There is no traffic on the street. The telephone seldom rings. Sundays always make me feel a bit strange.

I wake up before Jon, shower, and fix coffee. I read the most important sections of the *Times*: Magazine, Book Review, Arts and Leisure. I skip The News of the Week in Review because it's always too depressing (war, famine, plague, rape, abuse, corruption, inflation, recession, eco-disasters, and religious fanatics).

At ten o'clock Jon is still sleeping and I have about an hour before his alarm goes off. I gather my thoughts onto paper. Smoking cigarettes and drinking coffee, filling up empty pages, trying to make sense of my life, this world.

When Jon awakens he rushes to the bathroom, showers, dresses, and gulps two mugs of coffee.

"Good morning," I say,

"Good morning." His eyes are still at half-mast and he hasn't shaved yet. The rakishness of his stubble and demeanor are kind of sexy.

"Did you sleep well?"

"Okay."

"Good."

His aloof manner begins to cancel out the sexiness.

He packs his shoulder bag, says good-bye, and leaves.

I continue writing.

Less than a minute later he returns, with a doorknob in his hand. He hurls it to the floor and shouts, "I HATE THIS GODDAMNED FUCKING BUILDING!"

"What happened?"

"I tried to open the outer door and when I pulled the doorknob it came off in my hand and the one on the other side fell out. We're locked in!"

He paces back and forth, scowling, slamming his fist into his palm.

"You couldn't sort of stick it back in and try turning it?"

"I tried. It didn't work, goddamnit!" He dramatically studies his wrist watch. "And I'll be late."

"I'll call the Super," I say and fetch my directory. Fortunately, he's at home. He says he'll be over in about fifteen minutes. I relay this information to Jon.

"I HATE THIS GODDAMNED FUCKING BUILDING!"

I've been holding back my thoughts and feelings for too long. The pressure in my brain is impossible to contain. I dare to take the first step that could lead to disaster.

"What you really mean is that you hate living with me."

He stops moving. Stares at me. It takes him a moment to hear the echo of these words. And he realizes that the inevitable has finally happened. He stammers slightly when he says, "That's not what I said."

It's too late to backtrack. "No, but it's what you meant."

His face becomes tight, the morning softness is gone. "Maybe you're right," he whispers.

"Now that we've got this out, at some point – whenever you're ready – we can talk about it and figure out what to do."

"Okay," he says with bitterness. Then stands there, fists clenched, uncertain what to do.

"You'd better go down and wait for the Super or else you'll be late."

"Fine."

He picks up the doorknob and I start to shake. At the same time that I'm feeling relieved that this has finally been articulated, I'm frightened at the prospects. Will he be vengeful and destructive? Will I miss him so much it breaks my heart? Will this ease the tension or increase it?

I try to go back to my writing but my thoughts won't let me. Until Jon and I settle this, until I can figure out what he plans to do and how it will affect me, I won't be able to think about anything else. I realize that what I've just done will have a profound effect on my future. What remains of my future. Facing the unknown frightens me. A dark abyss opens before me and I can feel myself falling, rolling, tumbling in cold air. There's nothing to grab onto that can break the fall. I don't know if the landing will be hard or soft.

Jon won't be home from the matinee until about six o'clock. I still have to get through a long, slow, Sunday afternoon.

I decide to call Mom. A chat with her will be soothing, reassuring, will help to pass the time.

"Mom, it's me."

"I was just thinking about you! How are you?" Her chipper mood eases me right away.

"Fine. And you?"

"Can't complain. Except about the weather. It's too darn hot!"

"Same here. Hot and sticky. What's new?" I glance around the apartment and try to imagine what it will look like with Jon's belongings removed. Will he take the aquariums?

"Not much. I had dinner with your aunt and uncle last night. Sometimes they drive me crazy. Especially your uncle. He's such a – what do you call it – male something pig?"

"Chauvinist."

"Right. But family is family. And I spoke to your brother this morning."

"How is he?"

"He's fine. They're all fine. Have you spoken with them lately?"

"No."

"Alison is expecting again."

"I thought they weren't going to have any more."

"It was an accident," she sighs.

"She could have an abortion," I say, perhaps a bit more sarcastically than I intended.

"Forget it. You know her people don't believe in it."

"Yeah. They think women are chattel. And they go nuts when you talk about abortion but they don't give a fuck what happens to the kid if the parents can't provide for it."

"Watch your language."

"Sorry."

"You seem unusually bitter today. What's wrong?"

I brace myself and prepare for a lecture. "Remember I told you that things aren't going very well between Jon and me?"

"Yes. I've been thinking about it."

"Well, we're going to break up. I'm not sure yet what's going to happen – we haven't really discussed it in detail – but it looks like we're going to separate and all we have to do now is figure out how and when it's going to happen."

"Have you tried everything?" she asks. "It's never too late for apologies and making up. You know you can smooth things over and try to work on your problems instead of just giving up."

"I don't want to make it work. And I don't think he does either. Maybe we decided to live together too quickly. Maybe we're just growing in opposite directions. I don't know. But we never have sex. We never even touch. We never talk anymore. And the tension between us is so thick you can smell it. Maybe it's because the apartment is so small."

"Then move to a bigger one."

"He can afford it. I can't. In fact, that may be part of the problem. There's a lot of things he can afford now. He's really raking it in. And I'm still a pauper."

"If money's the problem ...."

"Mom, I don't want your money. I want out of this relationship. That's all."

"It's a jungle out there," she warns.

"What you mean is you don't want me tomcatting around like I used to."

"What I mean is I don't want you getting AIDS."

I guess I knew it would come to this. For a moment I think of the consequences of continuing to keep this from her. And then I picture a scenario in which I die suddenly and she finds out from some cold-blooded doctor.

"Mom, there's never a good time to tell a person something like this, so I'll just say it now and hope for the best."

"What are you trying to tell me?"

I can detect fear in her voice. As gently as I can I say, "I already have AIDS. What I mean is, I'm HIV positive. But I'm okay. So far. Really. I took the test, my doctor is treating me and that's really all there is to say about it at this point."

I prepare myself for crying, screaming. I wouldn't be at all surprised if she goes completely berserk. But without hesitating for a moment, she says, calmly, "What can I do?"

"There's nothing you can do. Except vote against the politicians who would gleefully watch me die."

"There must be something I can do. Do you want to quit your job? Come live with me? If you and Jon are really breaking up – do you want to live alone? You can stay with me. I'll take care of you."

I want to cry. Her concern moves me profoundly. Her calm, rational response is nothing like the hysterics I expected. If I were in the same room with her I'd kiss her feet.

"I can't tell you what a relief it is that you're being so strong about this. I thought you'd freak out. And that's not what I need. I need you to be strong and rational. Thank you, Mom."

"Don't thank me. Crying won't do us any good. But there must be something I can do. Treatments are expensive."

"So far, I'm covered by the medical plan at work."

"What's your doctor doing for you? Have you discussed this new drug, ZAT?"

"AZT. I'm on it. And a drug called Zovirax and another called Pentamidine. And there are newer, better treatments being tested. I'm hopeful that they'll be able to keep me alive until a cure is found." I try to sound convincing about this although I'm full of doubt and skepticism.

"So, you think now is the best time to break up with Jon?"

"I have no choice. We're making each other miserable. And I don't want him to stay with me just because I'm sick."

"Come live with me. You won't have to work."

"But I want to work. There's no reason for me not to. I don't have as much energy as I used to and I have my moments of despair and fear, but working helps keep my mind off it."

"I'd worry if you were living alone."

"I worry that *you're* living alone!" I say. "But life isn't always what we want it to be. If things get really bad I'll come live with you. But for the time being, I'm basically okay."

"If you need anything ..."

"I won't hesitate to call."

"You're sure?"

"I'm sure."

"Good."

"Mom, can you do me a favor?"

"Anything?"

"Can you tell Greg for me?"

"Why?"

"Because he'll get very upset. I just know it. He always goes haywire when I tell him bad news. He'll probably cry. And then I'll get depressed. If there are any tears to be shed at this point, you and he can do it together and leave me out of it. I need to think positive thoughts. A crying scene with Greg will stress me out completely."

"Of course, I'll tell him and Alison, but the kids don't have to know. And I won't say anything to your aunt and your uncle."

"Good. There's no reason to. Yet."

We say our good-byes, which, understandably, last a bit

longer than usual.

I hang up the telephone and a wave washes over me. Cleansing me of all the anxiety I'd built up. Telling a parent that you have AIDS is just like coming out of the closet all over again. The only thing scarier than the thought of dying was the prospect of having to discuss this with my family. I manage to convince myself that the worst is over. I try to think about other things.

I sit at my typewriter and attempt to work on my murder mystery. But I feel blocked. No words will come. I try to build images in the air, create a movie in my mind, but a stark blankness prevails.

Then a voice says, write it down.

It's Gary's voice. I turn and see him floating in a mist.

Write it down.

Write what down?

Your thoughts and feelings.

Gary, do you remember when we'd all get together and discuss each other's work? Those intense brainstorming sessions when matters of plot, character, atmosphere, and language kept us from our lovers and friends, the discos and bars, movies and television? Writing is such a lonely business. I thought I'd have my writer buddies with me forever. That we'd grow together and slap each other's backs when we were finally published, that we'd have someone there to point out the flaws so we wouldn't embarrass ourselves with agents and editors.

But first Ted died. Then Russell. And then Jay. And then Steve. And then you. And now I'm all alone. And my last day could come any time now. All I have is my typewriter and my fear.

Remember the party that Russell's lover had? I guess I thought it was inappropriate to throw a party for someone who's just died. But I have to allow people to acknowledge death in whatever ways they deem suitable. Yet at the same time, I was so exhilarated. Remember when we met Bill Whitehead? How excited we were to meet a prominent editor with a big publishing corporation? Do you recall how encouraging he was. How sweet and kind? I'd begun to think that all editors were monsters. But Bill made me realize that they're only human. And now he's gone too.

I feel so lonely sometimes I might as well be dead.

When I look at you now I'm so relieved that death has erased your deformity. When the lesions first began to appear on your face, I thought they didn't look too bad. Even told myself that if I had to cope with it myself, I'd be able. But as your face became more unrecognizable I began to get scared. I didn't know what to say to you. I was so grateful that you never mentioned it. That we could sit and talk and pretend that everything was the way it had always been. But I remember – so vividly – the last time I saw you. When we walked down the street, people stopped and stared at you as though you were a carnival side-show attraction. I hated them for it. My heart slammed against my ribcage as I tried to act nonchalant. And then when we sat down in the restaurant and the waitress approached our table I prepared myself for the worst. But she looked at you and gave no sign that anything was unusual. She took your order, then mine, walked away, and I wanted to hug her and thank her for being so kind, so understanding. But all the time I sat there looking at you I wanted to ask: how does it feel? Do you cry? How do you cope with it? What's it like to go from handsome to deformed in a matter of weeks? Do you avoid mirrors? But you acted as though nothing had changed and when we separated after lunch I cried when I got back to the office. Not because I knew I'd never see you again; after all, you seemed fine otherwise. I cried because I felt the weight of the burden you carried. I knew that if what happened to you ever happened to me, I couldn't be as courageous and dignified as you were. You were so brave and strong. Now, every blemish, every itch, every tinge makes me tremble in terror. I never realized before how vain I am.

Write it all down, he says, and drifts away like a cloud in the wind.

I try to hold back the tears. But they flow as my chest heaves and I sob like a jackhammer. I cry until I'm drained. Then wash my face and light a cigarette.

I force myself to spend some time with my typewriter and finally fill a few pages with words of anger and fear. Then I break away and move to the telephone. I call Dayna but she's not at home. She forgot to turn on her answering machine so I cannot leave a message.

I feed the fish. Watch them for a while.

Scanning the shelves, I gaze at some of my favorite books. But at the moment they all seem irrelevant, or too exotic, or scary, ephemeral, or too cerebral. I stare at the rows of record albums, hoping one will call out to be listened to. Anything to distract me and occupy my mind. Finally, I decide to leave the programming to whatever the radio is playing. I turn it on, look for something interesting, and hear some strange ethnic music from I don't know where. The vice that clamps my brain has loosened for a while. But then I hear the key in the lock and I freeze. Turning the radio down, I light a cigarette and try to prepare myself for the coming confrontation.

He glares at me, so I glare back. He says nothing, puts down his shoulder bag.

I finally say, "Hello." And though I try to make it as neutral as possible, it still comes out with a bit of an edge.

"Hello," he says gruffly.

"Has the doorknob been fixed?"

"Yes."

"Good. How was your day?"

"Not bad. Yours?"

"Horrible," I confess.

"Mine was, too."

"I think we should talk about it." I've shied away from this for so long, I find it hard to believe that I'm actually going through with it.

"Okay." He sits and lights a cigarette. "Have the fishies been fed yet?"

"Yes."

"Good." He waits for me to begin.

"All day long," I begin, "I couldn't think about anything except how unhappy I've been lately. And you seem to be pretty unhappy, too. I feel as though you despise me. And if that's the case, we shouldn't live together any more."

He's been staring at the floor. He raises his head to look at me and his eyes seem moist. "I don't despise you," he says softly. "I'm just not happy here. It's too small and there are too many problems. I want to move out. Get a place of my own. I've been thinking about it for a while, but I was afraid to say anything."

"Why?"

"I didn't want things to get any worse between us. I didn't want to hurt you. And I didn't want you to hate me. I still love you – I just can't live with you any more. Not now."

I'm completely stunned that he still claims to love me. There's been no recent evidence to prove it. "I can't believe you still love me. You've been treating me like your worst enemy."

"It's just that ... you're too tied up with your writing and I'm too preoccupied with my career. There's no room for an us anymore. Everything's changed. We're on separate tracks heading in different directions."

"That's the perfect description," I agree. "I've really tried to make things work between us. But I can't seem to find any solutions."

"I don't want to change my life for you and you don't want to change your life for me. It's as simple as that. We should accept it and move on."

I was afraid that he might fight to stay – or that I'd not want him to go. That one or both of us would cling to the other out of a sense of duty or obligation. Unwilling, perhaps, to admit that we couldn't make it work.

"I guess, then we're in agreement that the best thing to do for now is to separate," I say. "I just don't want you to feel like I'm throwing you out."

"And I don't want you to think I'm abandoning you. I just

want to live alone. For now."

"Where do we go from here?"

"I'll start looking for a new place. It might take me a while to find something."

"Take all the time you need." My pulse slows a bit, my heart lightens up. "I feel better already knowing that we finally talked about this. I don't want us to be enemies. Maybe we can still be friends." I'm skeptical, but feel that it had to be said.

"I'm so glad you said that. I still have feelings for you. I don't want to hurt you."

"I don't want to hurt you either."

If we continue to talk about this any more right now, we will most likely get maudlin and sentimental, or begin picking away at each other's faults. I change the subject by sincerely inquiring as to the matinee; was it a full house, were there any standing ovations, did anybody flub a line or an entrance?

He tells me about the audience, what went on backstage, who showed up with a hangover. Eventually we go out to eat, rent a video on the way back home and watch it together before going to sleep.

TWELVE

I'VE BEEN KEEPING ERIC'S PHONE NUMBER, on a crumpled piece of paper, in the pocket of my denim jacket. Every time I feel it I recall the night he tried to kiss me and I wouldn't let him. I dial the telephone and after two rings consider the possibility that I'll be talking to an answering machine or no one. But Eric picks it up on the fourth ring and when I say who's calling, he remembers me. This makes me feel very good.

"You said to call sometime. I think you meant if I ever needed anything. Well, I don't really need anything right now. I just wanted to talk to you and tell you something."

"Oh? What's that?"

He sounds too eager. As though whatever I have to tell him is monumentally significant, that it might benefit him somehow. I hope it isn't too much of a let-down. "First," I say, "tell me how you are. Is everything going well? Are you selling those computers left and right?"

"Things are okay. But I'm feeling a little burnt out. Ready for a vacation. What's up with you?"

"Well, remember how I told you about Jon and how we're not getting along?"

"Yes."

The way he says this I'm not convinced. But I press on. "We had a long talk and decided that we aren't going to live together anymore. As soon as he finds a new place I'll be on my own again."

"Great," he says, but so disinterestedly I'm not certain

that he's picked up on my hint. A vast silence hangs between us.

Finally, I say, "I'm free to see other people," recalling how he pounced on me when we first met.

"Oh," he says, not as excited as I had hoped. Did I overestimate his ardor? Was he just feeling sympathy? No. I recall that he pounced before I told him anything.

"I guess you could say that I'm old-fashioned. As long as I was committed to Jon I would have felt weird about seeing other people. But now it's over and I'm free. Available. I thought maybe we could get together one of these days."

I feel like I'm standing on the edge of a precipice as I wait for his response.

"Well, the fact is, I'm taking my vacation for the next three weeks. Starting the day after tomorrow. I'll give you a call when I get back. What's your number?"

I tell him and try not to let my skepticism show. I'm not at all convinced that he even remembers who I am, wants to see me ever again. But I wish him a cheerful bon voyage and hang up.

As the words of this phone conversation echo in my ears, I'm certain that I'll never hear from him. He didn't sound very enthusiastic. I shouldn't have called. What a fool I am. When he told me to call him if I needed anything he was just being nice. When he tried to initiate sex with me it was before he knew I'm diseased. How could I be so naive? I feel so stupid I could kill myself.

Within several weeks after Jon moved in things began to change for us. We thought of each other as good luck charms. My first short story was published in a respectable literary magazine. He got his first leading role in an off-Broadway play. It ran for almost eight months and he collected some very complimentary reviews. Jon played the eldest son, the only sane family member, surrounded by a mother with delusions of grandeur, a drunken father, a sluttish sister, and murderous brother. When that play closed he immediately got another part, in a comedy, about the denizens of an all-night diner in Los Angeles whose antics kept the audiences laughing from start to finish.

A few months after that play closed, Jon got his first Broadway part. As an understudy. But the play closed after three performances. And then he landed a meaty role in a revival of a musical, which ran for almost a year. During this period my first novel was published. Jon and I were happier than we'd ever been before.

My writing didn't earn much money. But I got some good reviews and was pleased with my progress. Jon's salary quadrupled and he bought a VCR, a CD player, a bigger color television set, eventually, the aquariums.

The major change occurred when he was able to quit his day job at the restaurant. Except for matinee days, he had to be at the theater in the early evenings and got home just before I would have to go to sleep.

At first this arrangement seemed satisfactory. I spent my evenings with my typewriter, Jon spent his on stage. While I was at the office during the day, he slept late and relaxed. We had sex less often, had fewer talks and meals together. But we didn't mind because we were finally gaining some altitude after a lot of hard work, frustration, and a very slow, gradual climb.

I never felt like I was competing with Jon. I thought we were cheerleaders rooting for the same team. That goals achieved and points scored would be mutually beneficial. We offered criticism and suggestions after experiencing each other's work. I was grateful when he'd point out an awkward phrase or a lapse in logic. And I thought he appreciated my comments suggesting that he might consider toning something down, or building it up.

But it eventually became clear that we'd become engaged in a contest.

One day, I came home from the office with a very favorable review of my book a friend had clipped and sent.

Jon sat on the couch, watching television. He turned down the volume, read the review, and without commenting on it, pointed out that his soliloquy of the night before drew a louder, longer ovation than was usual. I congratulated him. A few days later I presented him with another kind review, thinking it would make him feel proud of me. He read it and handed it back as though dead fish had been wrapped in it. I didn't say anything, although I felt a bit strange. Then I noticed that every time I mentioned anything about my work, anything at all, he'd always shift the conversation to his work. I attempted to alter this tit-for-tat format by ostentatiously not mentioning my work when he brought up his own. If he relayed a compliment from the playwright I would congratulate him and then tell him about some music I'd heard. When he produced a fan letter, I read it, smiled, told him I was very proud, and then mentioned a new film I wanted to see. I was trying to communicate the idea that I was not competing with him and that it was not necessary for us to match our accomplishments in a one-to-one correspondence. But it didn't work. All references to my writing always led to a confirmation of his acting. So I stopped telling him what I'd been previously so eager to share. He stopped asking me about the things I was working on. And I guess I became something less than enthusiastic when he would chalk up his latest accolades.

Communication became sporadic. Tension began to build. We started to argue and fight over everything, including the fish tanks. We stopped having sex. He would want it at night when he got home from the theater, when I was tired and ready to go to sleep. I wanted it when I got home from work and he was getting ready to leave. We never talked about this. I realize now that we should have. I was afraid to bring it up, afraid that it might lead to a fight. Perhaps he felt the same way. This was when I became a serious masturbator. I'd do it when Jon was at work. He was probably doing it, too, when I was not around. We haven't touched each other in about two years. And I've become a master of self-manipulation.

He began to neglect his responsibilities. The dirty dishes piled up. I'd constantly have to remind him that the rent was due. He seemed to enjoy making me wait for his half. But, for me, the worst of all was that he began to treat the apartment like his personal ashtray. He'd leave empty cigarette packs around, never move his cups or plates from the table to the sink. Dirty socks and underwear were left wherever he chose to drop them. He'd leave the television on all night, fail to put books, CDs and videocassettes back on their shelves in several instances he left the apartment with a faucet still running. It was hard to believe he'd once been neat and orderly.

At first, I picked up after him. I'd empty his overflowing ashtrays, gather his laundry. Nothing backbreaking or really toilsome. Just simple tidying up. But resentment grew within me like a cancer. I felt degraded. Not because I'm above cleaning the house. But because he had demoted me to a servant. I was no longer his lover, no longer his friend. I was there to see that the bills were paid on time and that the apartment looked presentable.

We slept together, apart. Spoke to one another with forced civility. Shared nothing except for a movie and a meal every Sunday.

The first year of living together had been wonderful. During the second, things became strained. The third was intolerable.

You were always there for me, Dad. When I needed to lean on someone you were so dependable. I wish I had you here with me now. Life is rougher than I ever imagined it could be. I need you. But then, I've always needed you. And I never felt that I could reciprocate. There was nothing I could do for you. And you did everything for me. If you'd lived longer, perhaps I could have been of some use to you when you became too old to take care of yourself. But the irony is that you probably would have outlived me. I could be dead in a matter of days, weeks, months. If you were still here you'd probably be looking after me. I wish I'd had the opportunity to return some of the love and care you gave to me. To try to show you how much I appreciate all that you did for me. I'll never have the chance. So I'm trying to tell you now. Can you hear me? I feel like I owe you something. But I don't know how to pay back the debt. Are you listening?

Mom says she's not going to play golf anymore. I couldn't believe it at first. But the last time I talked to her she didn't even mention it. She told me that she faked her interest in golf to please you. Is this true? Did you have any idea that she really wasn't into it? She sure fooled me. And Greg, too. We thought she loved it as much as you did. I always knew that she loved you more than anything. But I never imagined that she'd go so far to prove it. I know you loved her and appreciated her. But did you know that she would have done anything, I mean absolutely anything, to please you? It's the kind of love I thought existed only in movies and fairy tales. But it's real.

If you can hear me or see me I guess you know that it's over with Jon. It's for the best, though. I'll probably never have a love as long and as deep as yours and Mom's. But that's okay. Different people get different things out of life. I guess I'm not a great lover. But I can cope. Really. I'm doing all right.

Did Mom ever tell you about the time I cut school with Sharon and Mom found us together on my bed? You never mentioned it, so maybe she never told you. This is what happened: Sharon's friend stole some passes from the vice principal's office and gave a couple to Sharon. You remember Sharon – she lived on Hickory Drive in the big white house? You always said her father was one of the richest guys in the neighborhood. Anyway, remember how I'd go over to her house every Friday night to watch *Star Trek*? She always had a few people over and we watched the show with rapt attention, like it was a ritual or something. Well, Sharon and I always talked about collaborating on a *Star Trek* script. We'd write it and then send it to the producers to see if they were interested in using it. Of course, we were so naive we didn't know that television producers don't buy unsolicited manuscripts from starry-eyed high school kids. But anyway, Sharon had these passes so we could cut out of school for a while and not get into trouble. Mom was at a luncheon in the city and wouldn't be back until around dinner time. Or so I thought. So Sharon and I left school and came to the house. We were going to write, or at least start, a script. But we wound up listening to records and – I don't remember exactly why or how – we ended up on my bed, lying side by side, listening. And eventually we fell asleep. There was never the possibility of anything sexual going on between us. We were just friends. Both of us wanted to be writers. It was the most innocent kind of thing, we never touched each other. Really. Anyway, Mom got home much earlier than I'd expected. And my stereo was going full blast. So we didn't hear her when she came into my room to see why someone was playing my stereo when I should have been at school. When Mom turned down the volume we woke up. And needless to say, we were so embarrassed we couldn't speak. We had our clothes on, but there we were, side by side on my bed. Mom didn't yell at me. She didn't even look angry. She just said hello to Sharon, asked about her family, while I lay there, dumbfounded, trying to think of a plausible excuse. It didn't occur to me then, but I've thought about it since. I think Mom was kind of proud. That maybe there was something going on between Sharon and me. That maybe I was a typical heterosexual kind of guy. Did Mom ever mention this to you? It still amazes me when I recall that scary evening when I revealed my big secret. I know of people whose folks won't even talk to them anymore. And you were so kind and understanding. I really appreciate it.

Back in high school I was considered a radical. I started out marching for civil rights and then I got involved in the anti-war movement. You and Mom accused me of being un-American. But you were wrong. It was just the opposite. I loved America. I wanted it to be the best place in the world. Which is why I was so concerned when I felt that something was wrong and had to be corrected. Like racial discrimination. And the Vietnam war. No matter how hard I try, Dad, I can't be impartial. I'm not like Turgenev. I care too much. And now I'm even more radical than I was in high school and college. The government is trying to kill me and all of my friends. So I'm fighting back. It's a matter of life and death. I know you wouldn't approve of some of the things I have to say about the American government these days. But you would say the same things if you were in my position. The way you felt about Hitler, because you are Jewish, is the way I feel about Bush, because I'm gay. He wants to exterminate everyone who doesn't look at life in the same exact way he does. I thought variety was the spice of life. Maybe on some other planet.

So I'm thinking about joining this group called ACT UP. They're trying to get the government to help keep us alive. I know you would be shocked by some of their tactics. They embarrass politicians, stop traffic, close down government buildings, fill the jails, and clog the courts. I think it's working. Progress has increased a degree or two. Medical research progress, that is. Every day the media still tell Americans that gay people don't matter and don't exist – or that a few of us do exist and that we're all child molesters, drug addicts, communists, or sex-crazed rapists. You know I'm nothing like that. You know that I'm a decent person who harms nobody.

Speaking of drugs, you'll be pleased to know that I don't smoke marijuana anymore. I stopped drinking booze. Not that I was overindulging. I was always pretty sensible about these things. But I understand they can affect my immune system. Really taking care of myself. You'd be pleased with my new daily regimen.

Do you remember when I got busted for possession of marijuana when I was in college and came home for the weekend? The cops treated me like I was a junkie or something. Looking back, it was kind of funny because I was just a silly college kid who smoked a joint occasionally. And they had me in this holding cage with international heroin traffickers and murderers. I was terrified. But now it seems kind of amusing. When the cops first arrested me they thought I was a hardened criminal. But while they were taking my fingerprints and my mug shot I guess they could tell that I was just a harmless kid. All I had on me was less than half an ounce. And I didn't give them a hard time or anything. I co-operated. They eventually realized that they weren't dealing with a really bad person. I think they actually regretted all the fuss that had to be made over an occasional user of a basically harmless substance. It makes me angry that the media still classify marijuana along with the harder stuff. The only thing the American media is good at doing is ignoring the truth. I remember so well the morning of my arraignment, when you and Mom picked me up at the courthouse. I'd just spent the night in a tiny, stinking cell, after spending an evening in a cage with some of the meanest, toughest guys I'd ever been near. But I think I was more frightened at the prospect of facing you and Mom than I was by the criminals or the law. When the judge dismissed my case because I was a first-time offender I was only partially relieved. I still had to look you in the eye. And, I thought, beg for mercy. But you weren't angry at all. You were worried. Afraid that something terrible might have happened to me in jail. You never once reprimanded me for getting into trouble. You simply asked if I was all right and if there was anything I needed. I thought you might disown me or lecture me and yell. I thought things would change be-tween us. That you might never trust me again. But by the next day it was like it had never happened. You never held it against me, or even teased me about it. Thank you for being so understanding. I think about this every time I see an an-ti-drug commercial on television. I appreciate the way you treated me. You were always so kind and generous. I couldn't ask for anything more.

I'll never know what it's like to be a father. I love kids and I think maybe I could do a decent job of raising them. But I could never be as good a father as you were. I mean, are. You're still my Dad. You don't actually have to be here to keep influencing me. You taught me well. I'm honest, thoughtful, compassionate and law-abiding, up to a point. I stand up for what I believe, I'm independent and I've done some work of which you would be proud. I wish you were here to see the books I've had published. It would make you feel good. Mom reads them and likes them. I think you would, too.

I miss you. And I think about you often. I wish I could see your face and hear your voice. I wish you could hold me like you did when I was a child and tell me that everything's going to be all right.

THIRTEEN

THERE IS A RENEWED EASE IN MY TALKS WITH JON. When we ask one another how are you, we really mean it. There are fewer evasions and no hard, angry stares of defiance. We tell each other all the things we were holding back.

"You remember," he asks, "the actress I told you about, Maggie, the one who plays the housekeeper?"

"Yes," I say, pouring some coffee. "You want more?"

He waves his hand over the mug. "No, thanks. Anyway, she's been having an affair with Tom – my understudy."

"I don't recall you mentioning him."

"He's the real cute one who we all thought was gay because when he first came along he spent a few nights with Arnold, then had a fling with Carl."

"Arnold's one of the dressers, right?"

"Right. A real queen. He could teach Elizabeth a few things. Anyway, you won't believe this – Maggie and Tom are getting married!"

I love backstage gossip. "No shit! Why is it that all of these gay guys are suddenly getting married – to women?"

"So they can pretend they're not gay."

"Does Maggie know?"

"Yes."

"And she's still going through with it?"

"Uh huh."

"Doesn't she realize he'll be at the peep shows, the piers, and tea rooms every chance he gets?"

"She says she doesn't care. She says that their relationship isn't about sex. They have something *spiritual*."

"But do they ever have sex?"

"They're both pretty cautious when it comes to talking about it." All this talk about sex makes me wonder if Jon and I will ever do it again.

"Are they planning a big wedding?"

A siren, belonging to an ambulance, cuts through the air like a laser.

"Not too big. They only invited a few people from the show."

"You?"

"Yes. But I'm not going. It's in Connecticut. On my only day off. And I'm not really that close to either of them. I'll send a nice gift."

"So, this guy, Tom, does he think if he gets married it'll help his career or something like that?"

"I don't know what he thinks. All I can tell you is Ruth ..."

"The stage manager?"

"Right. Every time someone mentions the impending nuptials she does the theme from *Dragnet*. You know, dum-da-dum-dum."

We laugh. Jon smiles and I smile back. It feels so good.

"I have some more news," he says.

"What's that?"

"I found a new place. Almost. I haven't signed the lease yet, but it looks pretty good."

"That was fast. It took me months to find this place."

"The recession has changed the market. But also, I got lucky. When I told Ruth I was going to move out she told me that an apartment in her building just became available. Her landlord likes to lease to people based on referrals – he's wary of people off the street and he doesn't like real estate agents. So she told him about me and I went to see him and it looks like it's going to work out."

"Where is it?"

"Forty-eighth Street. Very close to the theater. I can get

there in five minutes – no taxis, no subways."

"Sounds good. How big?"

"One bedroom. Air conditioned. Doorman. On the tenth floor. Not much of a view 'cause of the surrounding buildings, but a lot quieter than this place."

"Great," I say. "You know, I'm sorry things didn't work out for us." I mean this sincerely and I hope he believes me.

"I feel the same way."

"But I think it's probably for the best." I look at him in a way that I hope will convey my feeling that I wish him no harm and really think that this is the best way for both of us.

"I don't want us to be enemies," he says. "I hope we can be friends." He looks at me with innocent puppy-dog eyes and I remember how I felt when we first met.

"That's what I want too."

He fixes himself another mug of coffee, asks if I'd like any more. I tell him, no thank you, and finish what's left in my mug.

"So, what's new with you?" he asks.

I'm about to say, not much, but then, suddenly, I feel the urge to let go of everything I've been keeping from him. This might not be the best time to bring it up, but I tell myself that I've been avoiding this for too long already.

"I joined ACT UP. Went to a few meetings so far. My first demonstration – against Bush at the Waldorf – is next week. It feels good to be active again. It's been a long time."

"You old firebrand. Once a protester – always a protester."

"That's me."

He laughs. I grin. Not too sardonically, I hope. Then I take a deep breath and say, "There's more."

"Oh?" He looks at me expectantly, his face composed, every hair in place.

"The reason why I joined ACT UP is because I was tested. I'm positive. And my T cells are practically a memory. I'm taking AZT and a bunch of other drugs."

It takes a few moments for this to register. He stares at me, open-mouthed, not knowing what to say.

"I'm sorry to have to tell you this. I know you don't want to hear it, but if I've got it then there's a strong possibility that you do, too. You should take the test and find out for sure."

He starts to shake, his lips come together tightly and his forehead creases. As his shoulders curl forward he begins to cry. Tears fall from his eyes and he sobs loudly. I put my arms around him and draw him toward me. Then rub his back and tell him everything will be all right.

"I don't want to die," he cries, and I get angry. What does he have to be upset about? I'm the one who tested positive. Where's the sympathy for me? But then he says, "And I don't want you to die either," and I feel guilty at first for thinking what I just thought, but then I feel better, as though we're in this together.

I kiss his wet cheek. "I can't tell you that we're not going to die because someday we will. But maybe, if we take good care of ourselves, we can survive until they find a cure."

"I don't want to die," he sobs. His body is vibrating, he screws his fists into his eyes.

It takes a long time for me to calm him. I feel bad for having yanked him into this new reality. But I know I had to do it. It would have been unfair to keep this from him any longer.

He looks at me earnestly, through eyes that are moist and red. "Why did you tell me right after we decided to split up?" He sniffles like a little boy.

"Because I didn't want you to stay with me out of pity. I felt that if we weren't happy living together that this shouldn't be the reason to continue to torture each other. Do you understand?"

"Yes."

"But listen, nothing is irrecoverable. You haven't signed the lease yet, right?"

"Right."

"If you want us to try again, I'm up for it. If you take the test and it's positive we can take care of each other. For a while, anyway."

"I don't want to take the test," he says petulantly.

"That's up to you. But don't stay with me because I'm the one who's sick. I'll manage. If you want us to stay together it should be because we still love one another and still want to live together – not for any other reason."

"I still love you," he says.

"I love you too. But that doesn't mean that we won't make each other miserable."

He nods his head.

"Think about it," I say. "Let me know how you feel. If you decide to stay, we should talk about what went wrong and figure out what to do about it. Maybe we can even do some of the interior changes that you suggested before you moved in. If you decide to go, we'll still be friends. I won't feel like you're abandoning me. I've been coping with this thing on my own for a while now. I'll be okay."

I wonder if he believes what I'm saying. I'm somewhat doubtful myself. Putting on the happy face is at best a temporary solution. Acting like Pollyanna while you feel terribly morbid is a real strain.

I complete the new subscription ad. It implies that if you miss a single issue of *Manmeat* or *Big Boys* you'll never have sex again, warts will grow on your nose, and your life will fall apart. And if you do subscribe you'll be happier than Jeff Stryker's jockstrap. After placing the final draft in a folder, I glance at the ones I wrote and rejected before arriving at the copy which will please Valerie and The Boss.

It's time for more AZT. On my way to the water cooler I hope that someone, somewhere, will invent a pill, a potion, a poultice to cure my ills. It occurs to me that the moment before I started fretting over disease, I was laughing about an advertisement. My life is like a chain of paradoxes, oxymoronic, sometimes dark and sometimes light, like Prokofiev's piano sonatas, a creepy melodic dissonance that captures the nightmarish qualities of my dreamscape.

I return to my desk and the telephone rings.

"Hello, this is Dick Riser, I'm supposed to call for an interview and that's what I'm doing right now, calling."

It takes me a few seconds to figure out what's going on. And then I remember.

"Dick Riser, how are you?"

"Okay," he says.

I flip through my desk calendar. "You're only about forty-eight hours behind schedule."

"Huh?"

"According to my calendar you were supposed to call two days ago."

"Today's the tenth, right?"

"Today's the twelfth."

"Jeez! I didn't know that."

"Well, anyway, here you are. Just let me hook up my tape recorder."

While I take the small audiocassette machine from my desk drawer and attach the mike to the telephone, I explain that the call will be recorded just so there are no disputes later when the interview is printed.

"Is that okay? You don't have to answer any questions you don't want to and I won't mention anything you don't want me to. All right?"

"Sure. I got nothing to hide."

"Great. Ready?"

"Ready."

"Okay, to begin with, what made you want to become a porn star? When did you first get the idea."

"I dunno."

"I mean, is this something that you dreamed about when you were younger or is it something that just happened when you got older?"

"I can't remember."

"I see." I settle back and silently groan. This is going to be a real chore. The guy has nothing to say. "Tell me, how did you get your start?"

"Some guy."

"What guy?"

"I don't remember his name. An old guy."

"Okay, so what happened?"

"What d'ya mean?"

"Did he approach you or did you approach him?"

"He took some pitchers."

"Pitchers?"

"You know, pitchers of me with my clothes off."

"Nudes?"

"Yeah, no clothes no nothin'."

"I see. And then what happened?"

"I dunno."

"Were they published in a magazine?"

"Yeah. What you said. They were published in a maga-zine."

"Which one?"

It takes him a while to tell me, "I can't remember."

"I see. And when did you make your first film?"

"My first what?"

"Video."

"Oh. A while back."

"Did you enjoy it?"

"S'okay."

"What do mean, it was okay?"

"The drugs were better than the sex."

"I see. What kind of drugs?"

"You know, drugs."

"Tell me, Dick, what's your favorite color?"

"Yellow."

"What kind of yellow?"

"What d'ya mean?"

"Pale yellow, bright yellow, greenish yellow, orangish yellow?"

"Just yellow."

"Okay. Your favorite food?"

"M&M's."

"I said food, not candy." I'm working very hard to keep the

exasperation from my voice.

"Pizza."

"Okay, your favorite movie?"

"I don't go to movies. I'm *in* movies."

"Your favorite music?"

"There's this song that they used to play on the radio a lot but I can't remember what it's called."

"Your favorite book?"

"Book?"

"Yes. Book. You know, what do you read?"

"I never read."

"What's your favorite television show?"

"You know, the ones where they capture criminals."

"I see. Tell me, Dick, why is it that in your videos you never suck cock or take it up the ass?"

"Huh?"

"In your videos, you fuck guys, right?"

"Yeah."

"And guys suck your cock, right?"

"Right."

"But you never suck cock?"

"No."

"And you never get fucked in the ass?"

"No."

"Why?"

"Cuz I'm not really into guys, see."

"Why is that?"

"I dunno. I like girls. Skinny ones with big tits."

"I see. Then why do you make gay videos?"

"It's a job. You know. The money, the drugs."

"Any thoughts on the AIDS crisis?"

"The what?"

I wince. "How do you feel about the gay liberation move-ment?"

"I'm all for it, I think."

"I see. Is there anything you'd like to tell your fans?"

He thinks about this for a minute. "No."

"Is there anything I haven't mentioned that you'd like to talk about?"

"No."

"Okay, Dick, it's been really great talking with you, thanks for calling, bye now."

I hang up the phone and erase the tape. This has got to be the most boring interview ever conducted. Besides, the readers of my magazines do not want to see the strings in the marionette show, do not want to know that some of their favorite porn stars are straight and stupid. If Dick Riser had a bottlecap's worth of brain cells he would not have revealed his true sexual nature. I want to call up my contact in Los Angeles and scream at him for setting me up with this imbecile. But I restrain myself.

I pick up the folder with the new subscription ad, walk to Valerie's office, and place it on her desk. Thank God I get to go home soon.

I miss you, Donald. And I miss your paintings. You were such a big part of my life. And now there's a huge void that nothing can fill. Why is it that Gary and Lenny can leave their graves and come to visit me? Why is it that you cannot? Or will not. Is that it? Are you angry with me? I hope you understand that the reason I didn't see you in the hospital was that your brother and sister wouldn't allow me in. I came as soon as I found out you'd been admitted. And I sat in the waiting room for eight hours. When your sister finally condescended to talk to me – every ten minutes I begged the head nurse to contact her – she finally came and informed me that I didn't know you well enough. That I wasn't close enough. I guess she didn't know that we were best friends for the last ten years of your life. And had been lovers for a brief period before. In actuality, I was a lot closer to you than anyone in your family. And I couldn't even offer you comfort at your bedside. I hope your final days were not too unpleasant.

Your brother and sister also decided on a closed funeral.

Only family members were allowed in. Roy and Sara and I stood outside – it was a private chapel on East Eighty-forth Street – and said our own prayers. We reminisced about all the good times we'd had with you. We felt so bad, being denied access. But we didn't want to push too hard, we didn't want to offend your family. We weren't even able to find out where you were buried. I saw Roy and Sara only once after that. It was too painful for us to be together without you. I haven't heard from either of them since.

Do you remember the painting you were going to give me? For my birthday? I remember it so well because the last time I visited your loft I fell in love with it. It was a still life of your studio, with rolled-up paint tubes dripping explosions of color. It had a kind of dreamy look to it. I told you it was my favorite of all the work you'd done through the years. I was really surprised when you told me on my birthday that it was mine and that you'd have it delivered as soon as you had it framed. I protested, if you recall. Such an extravagant gift! After all, you could have gotten thousands for it if you'd chosen to sell. I regret having to tell you that I never got it. I contacted your brother a few weeks after the funeral and told him that you'd been planning on giving it to me. I wanted it as sort of a keepsake. Something to remember you by, something to remind me of your talent. But your brother didn't believe me. He thought I'd made the whole thing up and was trying to rip it off. It hurt to be accused of attempted thievery. But there was nothing I could do. Your family never knew me. And I suspect they never really knew you either. Because after you died they locked up all your paintings in some vault somewhere. They should have sponsored exhibits at the galleries where you regularly displayed your work. I know you would have wanted that. You created your paintings so people could see them. But now they're sequestered, gathering dust, invisible.

I miss you. I hope you're not angry with me. I wish you would visit me now and then. But perhaps, one day soon, I'll be visiting you.

FOURTEEN

DEATH IS A WARM FUR PROTECTING ME FROM THE CORROSIVE COLD.

Death is a cool rain cleansing me of the eviscerating heat.

I don't want to die but death looks like sweet relief.

The world has gone mad and I can't stand it any longer. I don't want to know about another oil spill, murdered queer, yet another lesbian mother separated from her children by an idiotic judge. I cannot tolerate any more book burnings, exploding abortion centers, racial wars, drug wars, religious wars. There is too much hate, ignorance, bias. In a country where the media make heroes of greedy scum like Trump and Iacocca, what place is there for someone like me? Children are dying in gang wars and racists are stockpiling weapons. Television and newspapers empower corrupt politicians. Taxes rise and the quality of life descends.

I want out.

My body is failing. I'm aging so fast it's frightening to look in the mirror, see all the little bumps where there used to be unblemished skin. Not yet forty, I feel like I'm seventy-five. I cough a lot, get tired quickly, itch everywhere, my sinuses are always clogged.

If there is no other habitable planet to which I can hitch a ride, then I must look to death and all it has to offer. Peace. Quiet. Nothingness. No one has yet convinced me that angels or devils, pearly gates, or burning fires await me. There is a void, an emptiness. That is all.

I've been hoarding pills. I have my prescriptions refilled before they run out. If my doctor asks, I tell him I lost some. Accidentally dropped them. When the time is right I'll swallow handfuls of colorful capsules and tablets. Death will taste like candy.

And if that fails I'll contact the Hemlock Society. They advertise a program for painless death. I'll send for their brochure. And then there's always *Final Exit* and Doctor Kevorkian, if he's not yet incarcerated. I've got all the bases covered to find happiness somewhere beyond life. Beyond this decaying nation. Away from this dying world. Apart from my rotting body.

I call Dayna. Tell her everything I've been feeling. She listens.

"You need someone with you," she says. "I'm coming right over."

"I want to be alone."

"No, you don't. Don't move. I'll be right there."

I smoke cigarettes and drink soda, waiting for her. I don't dare listen to music, read anything, turn on the television, look out the window. Everything reminds me of pain and suffering. Songs about separation, books about obstacles, television shows about criminals. I sit still and try not to think. I attempt to empty my brain of thought. But I can't escape. I lean back from the dark pit and try to hold on to something. But the ground gives way. There is nothing to grasp, nothing to support me. I feel like I'm plunging, faster and faster. I get hot and cold and I can no longer tell which way is up. Dizziness overtakes me. I feel feverish and weak.

The doorbell shrieks like an air raid siren.

Dayna comes through my door and squeezes me so tight I can hardly breathe. But I hold onto her and I can feel the vibrations begin to ebb. I finally stop shaking and gulp air. She rubs my neck and shoulders. Presses a wet towel to my forehead. Sits beside me, cross-legged on the couch.

"I told my mom that I'm sick. Told Jon, too. He's moving out soon. I don't know where I'm going any more. I don't want to live and I don't want to die. I'm so full of hate it scares me."

She doesn't say anything for a while. I rock back and forth. She holds my hand. I don't know what to say. Her touch keeps me from falling any further. We sit in my apartment as tires screech, people scream, bottles break in the street below.

"Everything's going to be all right," she says. "Things work out somehow. They always do. You're feeling bad right now. But in a while you'll feel better."

Minutes pass. I look at her. Trying not to cry. Her facial muscles are locked, rigid, her eyes wide. She's observing me intensely, as though I'm a specimen on a microscope slide. She's ready to move into action if anything happens.

"So," she says. "You told your mother and you told Jon. How did they take it?"

"It was weird. She asked what she could do for me. He freaked out completely. I was expecting the opposite."

"How do you feel about him moving out?"

"I really want him to. I don't want him to stay out of pity. And whatever we once had is gone."

"But do you think that living alone is the best thing for you right now?"

"I don't know what's the best thing. I just know that I wanted him to move out before I found out I was sick. And I want to try to live a normal life until whenever I can't any more. As long as I can continue to work, shop for groceries, operate the coffee maker and the stereo, there's nothing any-one can do for me. Except hold my hand and give me hugs. Thanks for coming over."

She embraces me and I hold her tight.

"Do you want to do anything?" she asks. "Take a walk, go to a movie, are you hungry?"

"No."

"Okay, then. We'll just sit here and talk. But if you want to do anything just let me know."

"I'd give anything for a good laugh," I say.

"Didja hear the one about Jesse Helms?"

"No. Do tell."

"He wants to outlaw all abortions, except in the case of a fetus who is a practicing homosexual."

We laugh. Bellyshakes and chest palpitations that go on and on. Every time I think we're going to stop we simply glance at one another and start laughing all over again.

I'm feeling a bit weary now. It's been a long day and I'd like to get home, put my feet up, close my eyes, and just relax for a while. My shoulders and neck ache from poring over small print, hunching over the typewriter. I yawn. The intercom buzzes and The Boss demands my presence immediately. Adrenaline surges into my drugstream and my heart beats faster as I hurry to his office.

He sits on his throne, behind his big table, smiling like Jabba the Hutt.

"Valerie tells me you're guilty of insubordination."

I have to think for a moment, try to ascertain what he's talking about. To stall I say, "Insubordination? I wasn't aware that she knew any words of more than two syllables."

He chuckles. Then frowns. "You are to respect and obey her."

"I'll respect her when she's earned it. As far as I can see she just makes one stupid decision after another and gets in the way of the rest of us doing our jobs properly."

"Yours is not to question or analyze, simply to meet deadlines."

"Yes, sir!" I say in mock military fashion, offering as much sarcasm as my lips can manage.

"Where is the new subscription ad you were supposed to do?"

"On her desk."

"Don't lie to me."

"It's on her desk. I dropped it off a while ago. If it's not there it's because she lost it or is just trying to make trouble for me."

"I'll see about this."

He buzzes Valerie's office, asks her if it's there. She affirms that it is. His frown becomes a smile.

"Well, well, well, you seem to be on the ball today."

I don't say anything.

He reaches for an envelope. Lifts it and waves it around. "I have a letter here from a subscriber who says he doesn't like reading safe sex stories."

I don't know where this is going, so I remain silent.

"Tell me," he says, "what is our policy regarding safe sex stories?"

I'm tempted to point out that he's the publisher and should know these things.

"Some I use and some I reject. Some readers like them, others don't. I try to give them a balance. I don't use a story just because it's safe or unsafe. I make my judgments based on the story as a whole, not on any one of its components."

"Do you think we'd sell more magazines if we didn't use them, or if we used more of them?"

"I don't think that's what sells the magazines. It's the photo sets. The stories are probably a secondary consideration to most of the buyers. If we have hot models and good photography, professional quality color separation and printing, people will buy."

He lights a cigarette and talks around it. "I am hereby ordering you to not print any more safe sex stories."

"Why?"

He waves the letter at me.

"Because of one letter? I have an entire file of letters from people who want safe sex stories. Would you like to see them?"

He shakes his head, no, and continues to wave the letter at me.

"I also get letters from religious retards who say that our magazines are blasphemous and that we'll burn in hell. Does that mean we should stop publishing altogether?"

"Yours is not to question, but to obey."

I'm so angry I could grab his cigarette and stab it out in

his eye. Jumping to my feet I bolt from his office, slamming the door on my way out.

Stomping down the hall, I cannot conceal my rage. People stare at me with quizzical eyes. I pass Sheila by the water cooler. She grabs my arm. "What's wrong, honey?"

"The asshole," I blurt. "He just ordered me to reject all safe sex stories."

She thinks about this for a moment. "Why?"

"Because he likes to throw his weight around, keep me mindful of who's in charge."

"Don't you just love it when he cuts off his nose to spite his face?"

"He just wants to give me a hard time because I give Valerie a hard time."

"He's a fool. Don't let him get to you."

"He already has. I'm really pissed!"

"Calm down. Don't let it upset you. I know he's an asshole, you know he's an asshole, we all know he's an asshole. It shouldn't ruin your day."

I return to my cubicle and breathe deeply. I feel as though a wet leather band is shrinking around my cranium under a hot desert sun. Do assholes become bosses, or do bosses become assholes? I ponder this as I try to figure out what I must do to regain a semblance of self-respect.

There is an empty carton on the floor between the television set and the betta tank. It begins to fill up as I scan the shelves for books, records, CDs, and videocassettes that Jon left behind. Although the apartment looks very different, almost barren, I'm starting to feel better about Jon's absence. I miss our little talks. I still haven't become reaccustomed to having the entire bed to myself. I wake up huddled near the edge and must remind myself that it's okay to stretch out.

I think he felt guilty about leaving. He gave me many things that I assumed he'd take with him and I'd have to replace. The coffee maker, the air conditioner, the television set, the VCR. It's possible that he left these items behind to facilitate the move. But something tells me they are meant to serve as tokens of friendship, peace offerings. I gladly accept them. He assured me that he could easily afford new ones.

But there are books, records, CDs, and video-cassettes that I think were not intentionally abandoned, objects that he inadvertently forgot about, caught up in the turmoil of relocating. I pack them, seal the carton with tape and carry it down to the street.

From the backseat of the taxi uptown I see Sixth Avenue with new eyes. I haven't traveled above Fourteenth Street in such a long time, I'm unaware of all the changes. Old sooty buildings have been replaced by taller, shinier ones. Stores and restaurants that had become so familiar a part of the landscape have been supplanted by strange businesses with bigger signs, larger windows. From Sheridan Square to Rockefeller Center, the sidewalks are more crowded than ever, the traffic a slowly unraveling knot of congestion.

The doorman admits me, announces me, and I take the elevator to the tenth floor.

"Hi," Jon says, beaming, "glad you could come." He kisses me. "What's that?"

"Some stuff you forgot. At least, I think you forgot."

He has a new, shorter haircut. It makes him look younger. After opening the carton and hastily examining the contents he says, "I meant for you to keep this stuff."

"But it's some of your favorites – the Shaw plays you've had since high school, the import of *Romeo and Juliet* conducted by Previn, the bootleg of Hitchcock's *Rope*."

"I wanted you to have these," he says.

"I didn't know. I thought they got lost in the shuffle."

"No, they're for you."

"I didn't know."

"Come, let me show you around."

The first thing I notice is the neatness. The ashtrays are clean, there are no empty cigarette packs lying around, no dirty clothes on the floor. And I realize, I know in my heart finally, that breaking up was the best thing for us. His sloppiness was a sign of his discontent. He's happier now. I am too. If we'd stayed together any longer we might have eventually murdered each other.

"This is the bedroom."

It's about the size of my entire apartment and though it's bare of decoration, the walls are clean, there is no plaster flaking from the ceiling.

"Very nice."

"I haven't had a chance yet to shop for curtains or anything."

"I'm sure it will look lovely."

"And this is the kitchenette."

All new appliances including a dishwasher. My memory contrasts the upper-middle-class surroundings of my childhood with my current bohemian squalor and I wonder where I went wrong along the way to adulthood.

"A dishwasher! How wonderful."

"And this is the living room. I'm still waiting for the coffee table to arrive."

I sit on the new couch, opposite the new stereo system, huge color television set, two VCRs. His aquaria are set up along the adjacent wall.

"This is great. You've managed to get settled very quickly."

"Would you like some coffee, beer, soda?"

"Some cold water would be great."

He hands me a tall, clear glass and I sip slowly.

"How are you getting along?" he asks.

"Oh, I'm fine. I'm not used to being alone yet but it's getting better."

"I miss you," he says.

"I miss you, too."

I still think he's attractive, with his supple build, sculpted face, pleasing manner. But now I'm content just to look. No need to touch.

"How *are* you," he asks, referring to my health, afraid to

say the ugly acronym.

"Hanging in there. I have my moments of depression, but basically I'm just keeping very busy. I have my aches, pains, and twinges, but the doctor says I'm responding to the medication well. I've been writing a lot, almost finished with the book I'm working on."

"Good. How are things at the office?"

"I hate it. It used to be so interesting but now it's just a chore. I'd like it more if The Boss wasn't such an idiot. But who knows, maybe all bosses are idiots and I wouldn't be happier anywhere else. How's the show?"

"Great. Still packin' 'em in. But it's mostly tourists now. A few nights ago some Hollywood people came. They loved it and they called my agent the next day. Nothing definite yet but there's some interest."

"Congratulations. Hollywood. Wow. My ex-lover – the movie star."

"Stop it," he says, blushing, staring at the carpet in embarrassment.

"You deserve it. You've worked hard," I tell him.

Previously, I couldn't get him to shut up about his career. Now he changes the subject. "What do you want to do?"

We spend the evening together. Dinner at an Italian restaurant, then a movie. He wants to pay for everything. I let him pick up the check at the restaurant, but insist on buying my own movie ticket, the popcorn, chocolate bars, and sodas.

There are moments when we're hesitant, cautious, but also stretches during which the old easiness and familiarity are apparent. Both of us make several remarks to indicate that while we're content to be alone, we miss one another. Each makes a point of mentioning that although we regret that things didn't work out, it's good that we can still be friends.

When Greg finds out that I'm a plague victim he calls me, in tears, sheds all of his anxiety about losing me, weeps, begs me not to die. I'm his big brother and without me he won't know what to do, will have no one to lean on when he's lost his way. I comfort him as best as I can, something I find myself doing more and more when others should be comforting me. His constant reminders that I'm the older one fall on my ear a little strangely. I stopped thinking of him as my younger brother long ago. When we were children and lived with our parents the age difference seemed pronounced, and as I took each step forward he was there to observe and imitate. But now the fifteen months that separate us are nothing compared to the other differences. I live in New York and he's in California; I'm a poor writer and editor, he's a wealthy businessperson; he's married with three kids and another on the way, I'm divorced and childless; he's straight and I'm gay. I don't feel like a big brother any more. I feel like we're old friends who can trace our relationship back to the beginning of time.

He seems to think that my HIV diagnosis is an automatic death sentence, that this will be the last time we speak, that we will never see one another again. I hasten to explain that, while several years ago there was little or no hope for people like me, there are new treatments and the possibility for temporary survival. He doesn't really believe me, thinks that I'm just trying to cheer him up. But eventually the sobbing ceases and I alter the conversation. Tell him about my new book, that though Jon and I are no longer living together we've managed to maintain our friendship.

Greg tells me about Alison, my sister-in-law, about Carrie, Melanie, and Diana, my nieces, about the new house they're planning to buy, about the big pool they will have in their backyard.

We talk about Mom, and when I mention how much I miss Dad, Greg starts crying all over again. But I calm him, we joke for a while about aunts, uncles, and cousins, then the call is over.

I open a book, but before I begin reading the telephone rings again. A voice says hi and it sounds somewhat familiar, but I can't identify it.

"Who's this?"

"Eric. I hope you remember me."

Of course I remember him. I recall how sweet he was when we met, how handsome and attractive, and the way he seemed to not want to have anything to do with me the last time we spoke.

"Yes, I remember. How are you? How was your vacation?"

"Really nice and peaceful. Just what I needed. I was in shreds before I left. Now I feel like a new man."

"Great. What did you do?"

"Not much. Visited my folks. Soaked up some sun, caught up on my reading, watched soaps in the afternoons and sit-coms at night."

"Sounds like heaven on earth."

"Yeah. It was wonderful."

I don't know what to say next. After our last conversation, I can't imagine why he called.

"So, what's new with you?" he asks.

"Not much. Just muddlin' through. Really nothing to talk about. I already told you that Jon and I were on the verge of breaking up. It's over now. He moved out. We're still friends, though, amazingly. Life goes on."

"How are you feeling?" he asks.

"Nothing life-threatening yet. Just the usual aches, pains, anxieties."

"Are you free this Friday night?"

I don't have to think about it. Of course, I'm free. My social calendar has been blank for a long time. But if I acknowledge this I'll sound too desperate. "Just let me check." I flip through the pages of the novel as if it were full of appointments, as though I must make certain that there are no scheduling con-flicts. "Yes, I'm free on Friday night."

"How about dinner and the theater?"

This is too good to be believed.

"I have tickets for the new Lanford Wilson play, have you seen it yet?"

I haven't seen anything on a stage since Jon got his first Broadway part, and prior to that, I can't even recall. "No, I haven't. I've been hearing great things about it. I'd love to go."

"Great. Do you want to eat before or after the show?" he asks.

"Whatever's best for you."

"Why don't we meet around seven, go uptown together, then come back downtown for dinner afterwards?"

"Fine. Where shall we meet?"

"Choose a place."

"I can come over to your apartment."

"You remember where it is?"

"Yes."

"See you then."

"At seven on Friday, your place."

"Bye now."

FIFTEEN

ONLY FIFTEEN MINUTES LEFT BEFORE IT'S TIME to leave work and go home. My blood is simmering. I'm still outraged that the man I work for has no principles, no moral sense, no conscience. And completely unaware of the political ramifications that are a part of publishing erotica in a puritan state. Flipping through a stack of edited stories, I seize the first that is about safe sex. I check the intro, title, author credit, and pull quotes, file the invoice, then take the story to the typesetting department.

There are four terminals surrounding the printer, four word processors busily tapping keyboards. I stand beside Ricardo and clear my throat. He looks up, brushes his hair from his forehead. "What can I do for you, sweetie?"

"Have you finished inputting the stories for *Manmeat* December yet?"

"Nope. One more to go after I finish this one."

"Good. I'm substituting this one for the one you haven't started yet."

I hand him the manuscript. He reads the title and chuckles. "My dear, who came up with this fabulous title? 'Penis On The Half Shell.' I love it."

"The author."

"Neal Downe. Great name. Why the substitution?" He rolls his chair on ball bearings away from the terminal, lights a cigarette, offers me one. I take it.

"Just to be contrary. Just to see what happens."

"My dear, you seem upset. What's wrong?"

I tell him about The Boss's stipulation to reject the safe sex stories, and that I've assumed the role of guerrilla saboteur and will take complete responsibility.

Ricardo looks stunned. "You never create any problems around here. What do you think he'll do when he finds out?"

As the list of possibilities scrolls across my mind it occurs to me that nothing can harm me any more. The condition of my blood makes it seem like I'm wearing impenetrable armor. The worst thing in the world that can happen to me has already happened and I have nothing more to fear. No mere mortal can seriously affect me now.

"He might fire me. But then, I might just get a reprimand. After all, where is he going to find someone who is willing to work for so little and put out so much, take so much abuse, get treated like a naughty child. The only thing keeping me here at this point is the medical plan."

"I see."

"But chances are he won't even notice. He's too busy worrying about the stock market to pay much attention to what's in the magazines. But then, of course, there are the spies and hench-persons around here who might inform on me. But I really don't care anymore."

"I love it! Our own little Stonewall rebellion right here at the office!" Then he says, "Did you hear about Valerie?"

"No. I don't think so. What?"

"Well, after your meeting with her ..."

"You heard about it already?"

"Oh, yeah. Word gets around fast. Anyway, she was so angry she accidentally dumped a cup of coffee in her lap. So she has this big wet stain on her skirt at the crotch, right? So, Jerry in accounting, he's passing her in the hall and he says, 'Have an accident?' And she gets real embarrassed and starts cursing him out because she thinks he's referring to her bodily functions. So when she finishes her tirade he says, 'I just meant that you spilled water or something.' So she says, 'It's coffee!' And he couldn't pass up the opportunity so he says,

'Well, what else could it be? Everyone knows you dried up years ago.'"

"He really said that?"

"That's right."

"So, what happened?"

"She fired him. But then The Boss hired him back ten minutes later."

"Can you imagine? Can't you just see the look on her face?"

"I wish there was a videotape."

Ricardo glances at his wrist watch. "I'll get to this story first thing Monday morning."

"Have a nice weekend."

"You too."

I return to my cubicle and pack my shoulder bag. On my way out I say good-bye to Sheila, to Tony. I stop in Jerry's office and congratulate him on his verbal retort. And while waiting for the elevator I say goodnight to Rita.

I haven't been on a date in such a long time I'm slightly nervous. But in a good kind of way. All my senses are heightened, I'm trying to look and act in a manner that will bring respect and admiration to my companion and myself. Like a small-town girl at her first prom, I want to make a good impression, dispel any unfavorable gossip. Eric is at ease, looks relaxed and tan, the conversation flows between us naturally, without force. The Lanford Wilson play is witty and thoughtful, very satisfying, which stimulates our feelings of goodwill, the spirit of camaraderie.

We taxi downtown and dine at a new restaurant, one which Eric's friend recommended. Fine food, excellent service, he'd said. I'd heard that it's dimly lit and not too noisy. It measures up on all counts. Sitting across from Eric, I look at the complete picture before me – the smart, subtle decor, a handsome man at an elegantly laid table – and feel the contentment that was mine when I'd first come to Manhattan and experienced finally the kind of social life I'd only dreamed of.

Eric's face is simple, easy to take in. Jon's has more complex angles and planes. Now that I've spent a little more time with Eric, I see that there is more to him than good skin and fine bone structure. His eyes take in everything and reflect intelligence, perception. His perfect teeth and animated lips speak with compassion and authority.

After praising the performances, the writing, the enthusiasm of the audience, Eric tells me about his family and how rejuvenated he feels now that he's had a vacation. He apologizes for having been so abrupt and unenthusiastic when I called. Although I had felt slighted at the time, I tell him I didn't notice anything that would merit reproach.

The waiter arrives and asks if we'd like to see the wine list.

"None for me," I say.

"Same here," says Eric.

"Can I get you anything from the bar?"

We both order club sodas with lime. By the time they arrive we've had a chance to look at the menu and a blackboard with the specials.

When we're finished eating, we order cappuccino. The conversation has flowed smoothly. After splitting the check, Eric asks if I'd like to go to his apartment. We walk slowly up Seventh Avenue.

The night is hot and his apartment is cool. The first time I came here the Southwestern style seemed unique. But I realize that it's suddenly become very popular and I'm starting to see elements of it everywhere. We sit on the same couch where Eric touched me and I recoiled. He offers me a drink of water.

"I feel a bit strange," I confess, placing my hand on his thigh. It's warm and solid. "I want to have sex with you but I have a lot of hang-ups to deal with right now."

"Like what?"

"I don't want to infect anyone with what I've got and I don't want to re-infect myself. My doctor says that every time you come into contact with HIV it does further damage."

"My doctor said the same thing." Our eyes meet and he says, "There's something I have to tell you. Something I didn't mention the last time. I guess because I didn't want to add to your burden."

I remember how I cried in his arms and how he held me.

"I'm HIV positive too and I'm also taking AZT, just like you."

"You look well. How do you feel?"

"Nothing major yet. A few small annoyances that I'm dealing with."

He has beautiful green eyes and as I gaze at him I want him, as I haven't wanted anything or anyone in a long time.

"How about your mind? Do you go nuts sometimes like I do?"

"I have my moments. But basically I try not to dwell on it too much."

He reaches over and rubs my neck. "Would you like a massage?"

I don't have to think about the answer to this question. "Yes."

"Do you mind taking your clothes off?" he asks.

"No."

"Do you mind if I take mine off?"

"No."

I unbutton his shirt. Then my own. We stand, remove our pants and underwear. I stare at his body – trim, with hard surfaces, dusted with sandy hair on his chest, arms and legs. He leads me to the bedroom, lights a candle on the dresser.

"Lie down on your stomach."

He straddles me, kneading my shoulders and back.

"That feels great. Don't stop. Ever."

"You know, when I first started taking AZT I couldn't get it up but now I'm horny as hell."

"Me too. I used to be strung out on cocaine but now I'm strung out on AZT."

We laugh.

I topple him off me and we wrestle playfully. He tickles me, then, overpowering me, pins me down, chest to chest, cock to cock. I feel him growing hard against my stomach. He kisses me, bites my neck. I shudder and moan as our hard cocks rub together between us. Every nerve in my body is receptive and eager. He rolls off, pulls me to a sitting position. Reaches beneath his bed and brings up a jar of lube. He greases my cock, I do the same to his. When he grips me firmly, I grin, watching the flickering candle shadows move over his body. I hold him tightly. We establish a rhythm, stroking each other's cock. He moves back as I lean forward, then in the opposite direction. We're moving as one. I'm reminded of an electric train I had as a child – a handcar – with two male figures pumping the long double-T handle between them, moving the train slowly along the track. I feel the tension building in my groin. We increase our speed and intensity. Eric begins to quiver and moan. We both shoot our loads onto the sheet between us where they commingle into one shimmering pool of opalescence.

When the aftershocks subside, Eric says, "Come." We laugh and he leads me to the bathroom. We shower together, soaping one another – arms, legs, buttocks, cocks – splashing water, teasing. Then we towel each other dry.

Back in the bedroom, we change the sheet, then fall together in one another's arms. We kiss and hug, then sleep in a warm embrace.

I dream about the electric trains of my youth.

Jon calls, asks if I want to have dinner with him on Sunday night. We meet at our favorite restaurant. During our courtship we tried just about every Mexican restaurant in Manhattan and finally agreed that the best is a small, nondescript place on MacDougal Street. It became our first choice whenever we had the craving for margaritas, jalapenos, and coffee with kahlua.

When I arrive Jon is already seated, waiting for me. He

hands me a small package in gift wrapping.

"What's this?"

"Open it, it's for you."

"What's the occasion?"

"No occasion. Just a little something."

I untie the ribbon, tear the red and gold paper. It's a CD of the London production of *Miss Saigon.*

"I'm up for a part in this show so I wanted to hear the music and I liked it so much I picked up a copy for you. You'll love it. East meets West theme. Marco Polo, *South Pacific, Madame Butterfly, Pacific Overtures, Platoon.* A Vietnamese woman has a child with an American soldier. It's very interesting. Good songs."

"Thank you. But you really shouldn't have."

"Just a token of my appreciation."

"Look, Jon, you don't have to give me things for us to remain friends. I don't blame you for anything. Do you remember when we first met, what we talked about?"

"We talked about a lot of things."

"Among them, Melville, *Moby Dick, Billy Budd,* and how there is no clear-cut demarcation between good and evil?"

"Ah, yes," he says grandly, "the ambiguities."

"Anyway, I don't think you're to blame for anything, nor am I. We're equally guilty or not guilty. There are things we should have said and things we shouldn't have. We're both responsible. Okay?"

"Okay."

The waitress takes our order, we don't have to refer to the menus. When Jon asks for a margarita, I order a Pepsi.

"What's wrong?" he asks.

"I don't drink alcohol any more."

"Oh. If you ever feel that you don't want to live by yourself any more you can come live with me. I have plenty of room. You know, if you get too sick or something." He places his hand over mine.

I'm moved by his offer. "Thanks. Maybe someday I'll take you up on it. You never can tell."

Then he says, "Getting back to Melville, I saw something on cable the other night that I've been dying to tell you about." His former enthusiasm is back. It's good to see him so earnest and excited.

"What's that?"

"Remember when we saw the fifties film of *Moby Dick*?"

"Directed by John Huston, screenplay by Ray Bradbury."

"Right! Well, are you aware that there's an earlier version, shot in the thirties, with – get this – Joan Bennett and John Barrymore?"

"No."

"Well, it's the worst. I laughed all the way through. You will, too. They've tacked on this romantic theme ..."

"No!"

"Yes. It's so horrible it's great fun. Another example of Hollywood raping a classic."

He pauses for a moment, then says. "Speaking of Hollywood, I'm going there in two weeks."

"Really? What's up?"

"A screen test!"

"No shit? That's great. Are you nervous?"

"A little. But what the fuck. If they like me, great. If they don't, I've still got the theater."

"That's really wonderful. I'm very happy for you. But speaking of Hollywood raping novels, they also rape actors. Be careful. Don't let them buy your soul."

"I won't. Really. I've given this a lot of thought. I think I know what I'm doing."

"What if they tell you to get married and pretend you're straight?"

"I'll tell 'em to suck my dick!"

We crack up, and then discuss our recent reading.

I realize that this is a relationship I want to maintain. Although we don't have much else in common, this is someone to whom I can talk about all my favorite things. I don't know anyone else who shares my specific interests; there is nobody else who cares so much about these things. More than anything else, I want Jon and me to stay friends.

When he asks me how work is going, I tell him that I think I probably won't be there very much longer. After recounting all the stress and turmoil of the previous Friday – the subscription ad, the young guy running around looking for naked porn stars, the useless interview, The Boss's attitude, the safe sex controversy ....

"I can handle the job, but I can't handle the politics."

I feel like I'm starting all over again. As though a new day is before me after a long night of bad dreams. I felt this way when I left home and went to college. Then, again, when I said good-bye to Boston and hello to Manhattan. And had the same feeling when Amos moved out, and then again when Mike left.

I guess I'm a serial monogamist, not suited for more than one guy at a time, but unable, or unwilling, to sustain a lifelong marriage. My life is what I've made of it. And I won't declare that I have no regrets because there are many. But I don't dwell on them. I hope to learn something from my mistakes. Sometimes, I do.

My mind has become quieter. My vision less blurred. I can look forward again. I wonder, though, how much of what I perceive is merely a trick of my imagination. And moreover, how much of what I call imagination is madness. I don't really know what insanity is any more. There are people who seem to me to be horrifyingly insane, yet find success, attain power. And people who make a lot of sense to me who are shunned and labeled crazy. I don't claim to understand the workings of this world. I just keep trying to inch forward.

And I have less baggage now. I don't have to keep my thoughts and feelings bundled up inside. I used to be terrified of provoking disagreements with Jon. I was afraid to tell people that I'm sick. I'd cower and cringe in the presence of The Boss. Foolishly did I avoid dealing with the changes in my body, the truths about my disease.

Now I feel like a ship that's made enough stops and unloaded enough cargo to continue traveling without the ballast, the dragging anchor raised from the mud. I can sail in any direction, move more quickly, design my own maps, chart my own destinations. I might not have a long journey ahead of me. I might wind up shipwrecked tomorrow. But between now and then I will find satisfaction, create whatever moments of happiness I can, do whatever I desire. Without fear.

I lie in bed, my eyes open, staring at the odd shapes where the plaster has fallen from the ceiling. As with the stars in the sky, I can draw imaginary lines, make my own constellations. I wait for sleep to come. And dreams.

I close my eyes.

Stan Leventhal (1951-1995)

STAN LEVENTHAL, author, editor, and publisher, lived in New York City in the 1980s through 1995 where he died of AIDS. He is fondly remembered as a generous, genuine and passionate advocate for social causes and other writers. He was nominated for a Lambda Literary Award three times: for the debut novel *Mountain Climbing in Sheridan Square*, *Faultlines* and *The Black Marble Pool*. He published one other novel and three collections of short stories.

He served as a judge for the annual Bill Whitehead Memorial Award and was a member of the Publishing Triangle Steering Committee. His short stories and reviews appeared in *Outweek, The Advocate, The New York Native, Torso, Mandate, Exquisite Corpse, The James White Review* and *Gaylaxian Gayzette.*

In addition, his work appeared in the anthologies: *Gay Life*, edited by Eric E. Rofes; *Shadows of Love*, edited by Charles Jurris; *The Stiffest of the Corpse*, edited by Andrei Codrescu; and *Sword of the Rainbow*, edited by Eric Garber and Jewelle Gomez. The author was actively involved in the fight for literacy. His message to his readers: "Literature is crucial to our lives; reading is fun."

About ReQueered Tales

In the heady days of the late 1960s, when young people in many western countries were in the streets protesting for a new, more inclusive world, some of us were in libraries, coffee shops, communes, retreats, bedrooms and dens plotting something even more startling: literature—high brow and pulp—for an explicitly gay audience. Specifically, we were craving to see our gay lives—in the closet, in the open, in bars, in dire straits and in love—reflected in mystery stories, romance, paranormal and more. Hercule Poirot, that engaging effete Belgian creation of Agatha Christie might have been gay ... Sherlock Holmes, to all intents and purposes, was one woman shy of gay ... but where were the *genuine gay sleuths,* where the reader need not read between the lines?

Beginning with Victor J Banis's "Man from C.A.M.P." pulps in the mid-60s—riotous romps spoofing the craze for James Bond spies—readers were suddenly being offered George Baxt's Pharoah Love, a black gay New York City detective, and a real turning point in Joseph Hansen's gay California insurance investigator, Dave Brandstetter, whose world weary Raymond Chandleresque adventures sold strongly and have never been out of print.

Over the next three decades, gay storytelling grew strongly in niche and mainstream publishing ventures. Even with the huge public crisis—as AIDS descended on the gay community beginning in the early 1980s—gay fiction flourished. Stonewall Inn, Alyson Publications, and others nurtured authors and readers ... until mainstream success seemed to come to a halt. While Lambda Literary Foundation had started to recognize work in annual awards about 1990, mainstream publishers began to have cold feet. And then, with the rise of ebooks in the new millennium which enabled a new self-publishing industry ... there was both an avalanche of new talent coming to market and burying of print authors who did not cross the divide.

The result?

Perhaps forty years of gay fiction—and notably gay and lesbian mystery, detective and suspense fiction—has been teetering on the brink of obscurity. Orphaned works, orphaned authors, many living and some having passed away—with no one to make the case for their creations to be returned to print (and e-print!).

Until now. That is the mission of *ReQueered Tales*: to bring back to circulation this treasure trove of fantastic fiction which, for one reason or another, has fallen by the wayside. In an era of ebooks, everything of value ought to be accessible. For a new generation of readers, these mystery tales are full of insights into the gay world of the 1960s, '70s, '80s and '90s. And for those of us who lived through the period, they are a delightful reminder of our youth and reflect some of our own struggles in growing up gay in those heady times.

We are honored, here at *ReQueered Tales*, to be custodians shepherding back into circulation some of the best gay and lesbian fiction writing and hope to bring many volumes to the public, in modestly priced, accessible editions, worldwide, over the coming months and years.

So please join us on this adventure of discovery and rediscovery of the rich talents of writers of recent years as the PIs, cops and amateur sleuths battle forces of evil with fierceness, humor and sometimes a pinch of love.

The ReQueered Tales Team

Justene Adamec • Alexander Inglis • Matt Lubbers-Moore

More from ReQueered Tales

Mountain Climbing in Sheridan Square
Stan Leventhal

A series of discrete episodes among friends provide snapshots of one gay man's life. There are parties, concerts, dinners with everyday life – and death – interwoven in the rich story-telling. An actress, a painter, a set designer, a writer – all sweating and surviving in Manhattan, all scoring their first successes. Part autobiography and part documentary, artfully written, it details the lives of these creative people. Young and professional, they know there is more to life than money. There is trust and the sort of love that trades in deeds of kindness.

"Stan Leventhal instantly transported me back to 1980s Manhattan. I was there too. His brilliantly captured story was like dipping madeleine into a teacup." — Joseph Yvon, *Goodreads*

"Stan was a literary activist who always gave to, built and endorsed literature and writers. On this Sunday morning, all these years later, I can see still see Stan in his apartment window on Christopher Street, next door to the Stonewall Inn, overlooking Sheridan Square as he typed away." — Michele Karlsberg, LGBTQ publicist and friend

Leventhal's debut novel was welcomed warmly as a Lambda Literary Awards Finalist in 1988. This new edition features a foreword by Christopher Bram (*Gods and Monsters*).

The Black Marble Pool
Stan Leventhal

When you first notice it, something seems a bit unusual. Then it occurs to you that most, if not all, of the pools you've ever seen before were painted blue or white. The Captain's House pool is black. Not painted black. But constructed of black marble and black tile. The marble has streaks of white that look like lightning bolts in a black sky. There is a sexiness to this pool; a personality. It looks and feels like a warm, wet blanket, surrounding and protecting you like a dark, quiet womb.

There's a dead body at the bottom of a pool in the backyard of a guest house in Key West. Who is he? And what caused his untimely demise? Maybe it's suicide. Or an accident. But more likely – murder! And who's responsible? One of the guests, the people who run the guest house or one of those mysterious women in town?

"What a refreshing read! Light and funny, with some kinky twists ... perfect for your holidays, while you're lounging on a nice beach or near a swimming pool with scarcely clad hunks around you and a cold drink in your hand." — Dieter Moitzi, *The Stuffed Coffin*

A Lambda Literary Awards Finalist in 1991, this new edition includes a foreword by renowned LGBTQ publicist and friend of Stan Leventhal, Michele Karlsberg.

Like People in History
Felice Picano

Solid, cautious Roger Sansarc and flamboy-ant, mercurial Alistair Dodge are second cousins who become lifelong friends when they first meet as nine-year-old boys in 1954. Their lives constantly intersect at cru-cial moments in their personal histories as each discovers his own unique – and unique-ly gay – identity. Their complex, tumultuous, and madcap relationship endures against 40 years of history and their involvement with the handsome model, poet, and decorated Vietnam vet Matt Loguidice, whom they both love. Picano chronicles and cele-brates gay life and subculture over the last half of the twentieth centu-ry: from the legendary 1969 gathering at Woodstock to the legendary parties at Fire Island Pines in the 1970s, from Malibu Beach in its palm-iest surfer days to San Francisco during its gayest era, from the cities and jungles of South Vietnam during the war to Manhattan's Greenwich Village and Upper East Side during the 1990s AIDS war.

"It's the heroic and funny saga of the last three decades by some-one who saw everything and forgot nothing." — Edmund White

"Harrowing and sad, and very funny, *Like People in History* man-ages to bridge the unnerving chasm between the queer present and the gay past." — Andrew Holleran

In a book that could have been written only by one who lived it and survived to tell, Picano weaves a powerful saga of four decades in the lives of two men and their lovers, relatives, friends, and enemies. Trag-ic, comic, sexy, and romantic, filled with varied and colorful characters, *Like People in History* is both extraordinarily moving and supremely entertaining.

Published to acclaim in 1995, winner of the Ferro-Grumley Award for Best Novel, this 25th Anniversary edition features a new foreword by Richard Burnett and an afterword by the author.

The Book of Lies
Felice Picano

Bright, ambitious, and handsome, Ross Ohrenstedt is a high flier in the fashionable field of queer studies. He has just taken a prestigious university position in Los Angeles and has been appointed to oversee the collection of papers and works of a leading light of the gay literary salon known as the Purple Circle. Ross stumbles across a lost work by an unknown author and his quest to identify the mystery writer and achieve the glory of scholastic tenure unveils increasingly bizarre and unbalanced facts about a group of writers who in the 1970s and 1980s broke new ground in the creation of a gay literary sensibility. But the dark truth contained within The Book of Lies is even more startling.

"Felice Picano's *The Book of Lies* is a story rich with history – a history that Picano himself was part of and helped shape ..."
— *The Washington Blade*

"Based on Picano's involvement with the Violet Quill Club (which included Edmund White and Andrew Holleran), this is an absorbing Henry James-style comedy of manners about how even when some writers find their way out of the closet, others still get left behind." — *The Mail on Sunday*

With biting wit and a lush sense of place and character, Felice Picano's daring novel is at once a stylish mystery, a comical roman-à-clef, and a wicked send-up of the new Ivory Tower.

First published to acclaim in 1998, this new edition features a foreword by David Bergman (*The Violet Hour*).

The Family of Max Desir
Robert Ferro

It was a family dealing with old values, acceptance and death. Max Desir loved his Italian roots and hearing his mother, Marie, recount tales of the old country. And he loved his American family, his father John a successful self-made businessman in New Jersey. As he came of age, Max discovered something else he loved – men – and met the love of his life in Italy. Now, at age 40, the family is split: Marie and his siblings accept Max and Nick as a stable, long-term couple but his father John does not. When a needlepoint family tree is to be hung at Christmas, it's too much for John. Then the spectre of death enters as Marie rapidly declines with brain cancer. Loyalties divided, acceptance of family is re-examined.

> "It is a quiet yet disquieting book, beautifully crafted, deeply moving and almost coincidentally gay." — Michael Lassell, *LA Weekly*

> "An honest, eloquent and entirely original novel ... at once realistic and mythological, intensely personal and public ... a triumph." — Edmund White

> "Sensitive and original ... beautifully sustained and often disturbing ... at once deeply personal and universal" —*New York Native*

In this beautiful, haunting tale, told in Robert Ferro's clear, impassioned narrative, he created a classic.

Originally published in 1983, this new edition includes a foreword by fellow author and friend Felice Picano (*Like People in History*).

The Blue Star
Robert Ferro

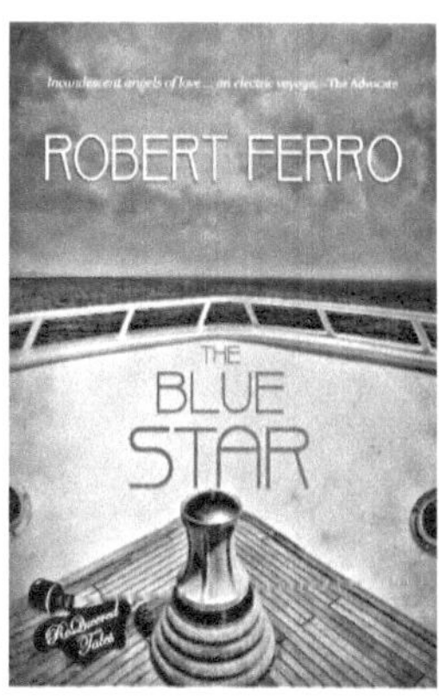

Two heroes, reflective Peter and Byronic Chase, indulge their youthful appetites in Florence. Over the next 20 years their paths diverge and reconverge. Chase marries into the Italian aristocracy and Peter pursues his passion for Lorenzo, a beautiful young Florentine. The past impinges on the present as the story of Chase's ancestor, Orvil Starkweather, is revealed -- the secrets of his life sounding a counterpoint to Chase's. New York City's Central Park and the imposing figure of designer Frederick Law Olmsted provide a mysterious connection to Chase's life. The story of the two men unfolds in Florence and New York exposing the unimagined and startling connection with the past, and taking them finally on a fateful cruise up the Nile aboard the luxury yacht.

> "A lush chronicle of the heart's education ... Ferro revels in life's ups and downs in a prose rife with pleasures rich as those described." — *Village Voice*

> "Enthralling ... euphoric imagination ... we can never forget the bliss we are allowed to share." — Richard Howard

> "Shimmering ... elegance, even if touched here and there by a measure of decadence, prevails ... superb taste and style." — *Publisher's Weekly*

Originally published in 1985, this new edition contains a foreword by Andrew Holleran (*Dancer from the Dance*).

Mysteries and More from ReQueered Tales

Body to Dye For
Grant Michaels

A Stan Kraychik Mystery, Book 1 – Stan "Vannos" Kraychik isn't your everyday Boston hairdresser. Manager of Snips Salon, which is owned by best bud (and occasional nemesis) Nicole, Stan thought this day was an ordinary one. A delivery van backed into the salon's rear driveway and accidentally spilled gallons of conditioner, leaving Stan and hunky Roger) embracing in a gooey mess trying to staunch the flow, with little success as they slid and slipped with Nicole watching on with rolling eyes. Later Roger is found murdered.

Stan's client, Calvin Redding, who owns the apartment where Roger's body was found, can't explain why the body is dressed in little more than bowties. Enter Lieutenant Branco, dark, muscular, Italian, (straight) of Boston PD Homicide who immediately suspects everyone, especially Stan. In an attempt to clear his name, Stan travels to California, takes up mountain climbing, eavesdropping, spying, schmoozing, and a little bit of schtupping, all in an attempt to find the truth.

"A delightful debut with a gay hairdresser-investigator who gets his fingers into a lot more things than hair. It's a promising start to what looks to be a successful series." — George Baxt, *The Dorothy Parker Murder Case*

Nominated for aLambda Literary Award. For this new edition, Carl Mesrobian reminisces about his brother Grant in an exclusive foreword, and Neil S. Plakcy provides an introduction of appreciation.

ReQueered Tales is publishing the complete series of six novels featuring Stan Kraychik through 2021.

Let's Get Criminal
Lev Raphael

A Nick Hoffman / Academic Mystery, Book 1 –Nick Hoffman has everything he has ever wanted: a good teaching job, a nice house, and a solid relationship with his lover, Stefan Borowski, a brilliant novelist at the State University of Michigan. But when Perry Cross shows up, Nick's peace of mind is shattered. Not only does he have to share his office with the nefarious Perry, who managed to weasel his way into a tenured position without the right qualifications, he also discovers that Perry played a destructive role in Stefan's past. When Perry turns up dead, Nick wonders if Stefan might be involved, while the campus police force is wondering the same about Nick.

> "*Let's Get Criminal* is a delightful romp in the wonderfully petty and backbiting world of academia. Well-drawn characters make up a delicious list of suspects and victims." — Faye Kellerman

> "Reading *Let's Get Criminal* is like sitting down for a good gossip with an old friend. Its instant intimacy and warmth provides clever and sheer fun." — Marissa Piesman

Originally published in 1996, this first book in the Nick Hoffman Academic Mystery series contains a new foreword by the author.

Also available in this series:

The Edith Wharton Murders

Nick Hoffman, desperate to get tenure, has been saddled with a thankless task: coordinating a conference on Edith Wharton that will demonstrate how his department and his university supports women's issues.

The Death of a Constant Lover

When the son of a professor is murdered on a campus bridge, Nick's presence at the scene puts him right where he can't afford to be: in the middle of trouble.

Murder and Mayhem
Matt Lubbers-Moore

An Annotated Bibliography of Gay and Queer Males in Mystery, 1909-2018.

Librarian and scholar Matt Lubbers-Moore collects and examines English language mystery novels that include a gay or queer male starting with the 1909 Arthur Conan Doyle short story "The Man with the Watches," which is included in its entirety. Authors, titles, dates published, publishers, book series, short blurbs, and a description of how involved the gay or queer male character is with the mystery are all included for a full bibliographic background.

> "The list is carefully parsed ... a brilliant reference book. Don't wait for the movie, or even an engaging discussion at your next visit to a gay bar. It is as useful as you want." — *Rainbow Book Reviews*

Murder and Mayhem will prove invaluable for mystery collectors, researchers, libraries, general readers, aficionados, bookstores, and devotees of LGBTQ studies. The bibliography is laid out in alphabetical order by author including the blurb and author notes, whether a hard boiled private eye, an amateur cozy, a suspenseful romance, or a police procedural. All subgenres within the mystery field are included: fantasy, science fiction, espionage, political intrigue, crime dramas, courtroom thrillers, and more with a definition guide of the subgenres for a better understanding of the genre as a whole.

Finalist at International Book Awards, Non-fiction, 2020.

A ReQueered Tales Original Publication.

ɷ

**If you enjoyed this book,
please help spread the word
by posting a short,
constructive review at
your favorite social media site
or book retailer.**

**We thank you, greatly,
for your support.**

And don't be shy! Contact us!

*For more information about current and future releases,
please contact us:*

E-mail: *requeeredtales@gmail.com*
Facebook (Like us!): www.facebook.com/ReQueeredTales
Twitter: @ReQueered
Instagram: www.instagram.com/requeered
Web: www.ReQueeredTales.com
Blog: www.ReQueeredTales.com/blog
Mailing list (Subscribe for latest news): https://bit.ly/RQTJoin